THE VOYAGES OF CINRAK THE DAPPER
A.J. Fitzwater

Copyright © 2020 by A.J. Fitzwater
ISBN 978-1-7325833-8-2

Library of Congress Control
Number: 2020930232

Queen of Swords Press LLC
Minneapolis, MN
www.queenofswordpress.com
Published in the United States

Cover Design by Dian Huynh of RubyDianArts
Interior Design and Cover Lettering by Terry Roy

"Wild Ride of the Untamed Stars" previously appeared in
Beneath Ceaseless Skies, Issue 252, May 24, 2018.

"Search for the Heart of the Ocean" previously appeared
in *Scourge of the Seas of Time (and Space)* edited by Catherine
Lundoff. Queen of Swords Press, 2018.

THE
VOYAGES OF
CINRAK
THE DAPPER

A.J. FITZWATER

CONTENTS

For the wary, weary traveller
Rest a while.

INTRODUCTION

J OY IS POLITICAL.

This is something I have come to understand as the political landscape has shifted in New Zealand and around the world, especially since 2016.

This is not a new idea, as all marginalized populations have found ways to continue despite the spirit being under duress, the body under threat, their words suppressed, their future in jeopardy. We tell joyful stories in times of fear to light the way in the dark, to document that history, to model the voices that need to be heard and the bodies that need to be seen, and to simply say *no*, you will *not* take our joy from us.

It has taken me a long time to understand why I write what I do. At first it was a simple human wish to find my voice. Then as my stories took a political and often very serious bent, it was about being part of reframing feminist and queer narratives for new generations and revisiting forgotten and neglected histories. Again, nothing new – staying on that learning journey keeps my soul nourished.

But what is new in the last decade or so is the propaganda landscape, the pace of news, a literal constant barrage in an information war that targets your empathy centre and punishes joy. Community and kindness, matriarchal, feminist, and indigenous frameworks that are proven strengths in the fight against the patriarchy, are weaponized by those scared of that power. 'Why are you worried about *this* when women over *there* have it so much worse?' 'Be grateful we *give* you *these* rights, because queer people over *there* don't have any.' Shootings, attacks, threats, abuse, aggressions macro and micro, bills and hate groups chipping away at LQBTQIA and reproductive rights and bodily autonomy...the onslaught is *supposed* to be Too Much.

When we grow tired within the fight, we step back and let another step up until we're ready to join the fight again. This is Cinrak's moment to put her best paw forward.

When I would tell people what I was writing, their faces would light up, they'd laugh, they'd express what a cute and fun juxtaposition that was. Rat pirates are a thing in fantasy, but capybaras, known in the real world for their chill and respect for other species? That put a spin on things.

This all seems rather serious for an introduction to a collection of stories about a lesbian capybara pirate and her found family, but I had to come to a place of understanding that this book is serious about its joy. I was initially bemused my first published book wasn't the srs bznss I'd originally intended when I started this writing journey years ago. Then I realized speaking to joy in times of turmoil, of being open about queer lives when others seek to supress those voices, *is* serious business when framed in terms of hope, respect, community organizing, and being able to see of oneself in the past, future, and present.

Come for handsome, huggable Cinrak in a dapper three-piece, stay for her becoming a house-ship Mother to an enormous found family, the ethical polyamory, trans boy chinchilla, genderqueer rat mentor, fairy, and whale, drag queen mer, democratic monarchy, socialist pirates, and strong unionization.

Because if the patriarchy is going to come at us for exposing their unearned privilege, for showing identity *is* political, we'll make sure our joy — our stories, rise, uplift — is political too.

Young Cinrak

Tail the First:
In Which Our Hero Discovers the
Price of Her Salt

THE FIZZLE STARTED LOW in Cinrak's stout belly. It wove around her ribs, along her spine, and ruffled the fur on the back of her neck.

Teetering atop the orphanage's great oak, the capybara instinctively turned her broad snout towards the silver sliver of harbour glimpsed through the straight-backed buildings of Ratholme. The oak tried to be as tall and graceful as possible for its charge, revelling at being a stand in for a pirate ship.

Cinrak shaded her eyes like she'd seen captains do. Dolphins? Wrong. An oncoming storm? No. The steady, warm nor'east wind had no intention of giving up its turn to its siblings.

Ah! There! Cutting around the headlands.

"Ship ahoy!" whisper-cried Cinrak to her 'crew' of oak leaves, who all shivered with anticipation.

5

What a beauty. For the purple thistle on white flag to be seen, the masts must be the tallest in the pirate fleet.

The harbour horns honked welcome, a harmony to the hammering of Cinrak's heart. She didn't recognize the complicated cadence, but it sang of just the importance Cinrak sought.

Could this be *her* ship?

As she did twice a sun since she ticked over into her fourteenth star-turn at the orphanage, she assessed her memorized packing list. A well-read, clean and handsome pirate was a good pirate, in Cinrak's estimation. www ♡

She wouldn't pack any of those awful frilly dresses Helet made her wear.

It wasn't running away to sea. Taking one's dream by the shoulders, speaking the words of apprenticeship with a clear and fierce voice, was a *plan*.
inspiring copy!
The kitchen door smacked open and the oak winced in sympathy for the courtyard wall.

"Cinrak, sweetheart!"

Cinrak winced at the endearment.

Helet did not look up. She never looked up.

"Cinrak, darling. I need you to go down to the bookseller and the library." The stout capybara matron stuck her head in the stables and the cool store. "Cinrak? Time to stop playing sillies now." 🙄

Cinrak landed with a thump-clatter on the cobbles. Helet reeled back, forepaw to chest. "Cinrak! Dearest!

Your dress! What would any of the anyone think if they saw you up there?"

Nothing, Cinrak presumed. Visitors to Helet's orphanage weren't interested in a loud voiced capybara who looked like a walking brick in a dress. All her friends of her age had already gone to apprenticeships or higher school. Some had even found families. — How ity...

As Helet rattled on with her instructions, Cinrak rolled the word around in her mind: *Family*. Hers had_ Omfg no!! been lost to a terrible influenza which had overtaken Ratholme just before Queen Lyola took the throne. She had been just a kit in arms, and what did names and faces of her herd mean if she didn't remember them? She preferred to dream forwards, not backwards, of her pirate family. They didn't have to be capybara either. She liked all species. Unlike Queen Lyola, who favoured rats above all, making things difficult at court, in trade, and in the streets. Wasn't that what a good pirate did? Fight for the downtrodden and meek _ hell yeah as well as the strong and silent?

Helet said her family was her and the orphanage kits, but it seemed more like Cinrak was the one acting like a mother before she even knew what being a kit meant. While Helet was busy giving sermons or lectures on her theological pride and joy, the Great WHAT. YES Capybara Mother, Cinrak was soothing nightmares aw.. and scraped knees. That felt more like work, especially when those young ones found a family and forgot her quick.

"Cinrak? Sweetie? Are you listening to me? Get your head out of the clouds." Helet folded her arms across her barrel chest. How did she manage to make dresses sit so nice on her broad frame? Cinrak couldn't understand how they were of the same species. "Did you get all that?"

Cinrak counted off on her claws. "Requests to the library. Payment for the bookseller, divided based on the rarity of the book. First dibs on whatever comes off the new ship. Apothecary for cough medicine, analgesic powder, and herbs for Marilette's fever. And absolutely *no* detours past the docks."

Ah, the exchange of information. Going to collect books. This wasn't *work*. That was an adventure worthy of a budding pirate.

"Good." Helet nodded stiffly, lifting her voice for the neighbours to hear. "No kit of mine will be seen near that den of dull-skuggery and delinquency."

Cinrak grimaced into the ruffles of her collar and edged towards the gate.

"And change your shoes, for Mother's sake," Helet sighed. "Those boots have mud all over them, and they don't go with that dress at *all*."

"'Come as you are, you fit and feeble, dirty and deterge, you are all welcome in my kenning'," Cinrak muttered, but Helet chose not to hear that particular quote from the Mother's Text.

HUNCHED IN THE OVERHANG of the market arch—it had only taken two tries to hoist herself up—Cinrak stewed over the questions she didn't have answers to, and might never.

Why had Helet chosen to be an orphanage matron? Was it the good stipend from crown and council? Rumour had it Queen Lyola disdained kits, more especially those who weren't rats, but she kept up appearances. Kits had repurposed an old rhyme, chanting in the markets "Lyola, Lyola, Lemon Face, be so ugly even cats won't chase." But even though Helet spoke fondly of the rat queen, especially in earshot of influential neighbours, she had yet to be invited to deliver a lecture on the Great Mother at court.

Ugh, her *lectures*. Cinrak felt like her fur would melt from boredom. Perhaps Helet chose the matronage life to have a dedicated congregation. "Get them young," as she said about pirates.

Cinrak wanted to talk about these Very Important Things, but Helet said she had to wait until she was grown up. On the other paw, Helet was always tasking her with Grown Up—boring—jobs, telling her to grow up, be a young *lady*, stop climbing the oak. Ugh. At *Rebel!!* what point was Grown Up *enough*?

She took a bite of her stolen green apple, and her spirits lifted. Today's lightpaw attempt was a win! Foncruter had marked her a solid six out of ten when she went back to pay. The ex-pirate who taught her these tricks had never given her anything above a five before. Why anyone would give up piratry for selling produce, Cinrak did not understand, though she did enjoy the air of mystery around the old ferret.

As she left, Foncruter's granddaughter Cassilly had blushed in her general direction. Cinrak didn't know how she made young girls blush, but she did, and she enjoyed it. *Omg*

The docks bustled to bursting point. People in frilly clothes conducted business discreet, frivolous, wanton, or intriguing depending on the agent's intent. The fishmongers called barter shanties, throwing wrapped fish to customers. The taverns were already bursting with cheer, sea paws searching for a good meal and a bath. Shouts ahoy guided crates of wondrous stuffs from afar onto carts.

This really is copy Redwall and I'm here for it

Somewhere in that mess *must* be the person who would teach Cinrak how to pirate, to fight and to curse.

Helet's stockist of esteemed theological texts had not received their shipment yet. The ship had barely begun unloading, and non-perishables were well down the list.

What a shame, Cinrak thought. She would just have to find another way to procure Helet's textbooks.

Ah, there!

A rat stood at the bottom of the gangplank, twirling their tail. Every now and then they'd toss an inventive curse at the handlers or squint at the frenetic activity surrounding one of the more salacious taverns, but otherwise boredom was writ large on their rusty brown features.

Cinrak triple-checked her garb. With her baggy pants tucked into boots, frilly, if frayed, shirt, and a belt with an oversized silver buckle (procured from the Theatre Rat-oyal's scrap bin), she thought she made a passable cabin kit.

Cinrak scrambled down, stood as straight as the oak had taught her, took a deep breath, then sauntered into the crowd. Exhilaration bubbled in her belly much like her strange fizzle. She was one of them, a real pirate, blending like salt into the ocean!

The bored rat looked Cinrak up and down with one keen eye, the other a silver scar from hairline to jaw. Stripped of her fur, Cinrak shivered.

"Greets. Yer a bit young to be 'round here." Their voice was rough and warm like a summer storm.

All feeling left Cinrak's tongue. "Old enough. Business. To be doing with. Likes of you."

A knife-like smile slid across the rat's face, twisting the scar. The sun hustled from behind a cloud, making everything too sharp. Shadows once warm with promise now were cold flashes with watchful eyes. The water slapped against the dock and ship impatiently. Ropes creaked warily.

The rat's smile softened, and the world snapped back into a single frame. "Eh, alright smarty pants. I

oh SNAP

like a sharp tongue on a young 'un. Shows they got wit." They held out a forepaw. "I be Mereg."

Sweet, delicious air flooded Cinrak's broad chest.

The rat hadn't given a gender signifier, so she switched her own dialect to Civil, to give her own gender signifier. "My name is Cinrak. Don't have any other name."

Having practised with the oak, she grasped Mereg's paw firmly, but the pi-rat switched the greeting, clasping wrists.

"That be the pirate way. Cinrak, eh? No other name by design or because ye still choosin'?"

"Because I didn't get one." One could *choose* a name? Helet said names were ordained by the Great Capybara Mother, and stuck for life.

"Aye, understood lass." Mereg wrapped their very long tail around their wrist. This close, Cinrak could see a light dusting of silver in their ear fluff too. "Now, what busy-ness you be wantin' with the *Cry Havoc*, feared by many, home to the loyal, decent few."

Cinrak loved pirate ship names, and this one was a beauty! The vessel was a wonder of rock candy, railings sunset yellow atop planks of midnight purple, doors and roofing blood red. The colours were not affectations of paint jobs renewed each season, but ingrained in the wood. A mer figurehead pinned the whole ship together, red hair whipping, green eyes shrewd and far-seeing.

"I have, uh, a client very interested in any books you have in your inventory. About theology. The Great Capybara Mother in particular."

"The Great Mother, eh?" Mereg eyeballed Cinrak like they were stripping the meat from her bones. ᴼᵂ They rubbed the digits of one paw together. "An' what sorta fee we talkin' if I let ye be first to dig through them crates."

Pirates will be pirates.

"Five percent above what you'd sell them to market."

The words shot out like Cinrak practised. She marvelled at how the rat, someone low in the crew to be pulling watch like this, kept a sloth-face.

"Ten."

"Six."

"Seven."

"Seven, with first look at your next shipment."

Mereg smirked. "Ye pretty good at this for a young 'un. Almost think ye got a bit o' pirate blood in ye."

Cinrak's spine crickled as she stood tall.

"A'ight." Mereg held out their paw again. "Ye have a deal. Come aboard, an' let's get crackin'."

Cinrak's rear paws tingled like the ship itself welcomed her on board.

"Ye ever bin on a pirate ship before, lass?" Mereg squinted as they descended into the gloomy hold.

Good pirates needed a little dastardliness. But Helet said good girls weren't liars. She wasn't a good girl for coming aboard the ship. She couldn't imagine such regret. How could one know their truth until one experienced it? Grown-ups could be so stupid.

"Nay." Cinrak gave in to her better side. "Treated with traders with my matron, but never been up close."

Mereg nodded. "Second rule of the ship is honesty. I appreciate that. If yer ma wants to have at about it, she can come to the Cap'n first."

"Not me ma," Cinrak muttered. Helet facing up to a pirate captain? That would be a treat!

"What that, lass?"

"I said, what's the first rule?"

"Loyalty to yer crew." Mereg adjusted some fairy-glow lamps to brighten their hue.

"Doesn't that cause conflict because everyone has different ideas and opinions?"

"Yer a sharp one. Aye, it does. The Cap'n appreciates that in the crew. We all have to work an' live an' sleep in the same space. Gotta be comfortable in consensus."

"Queen Lyola could learn a thing or two from pirates," Cinrak muttered.

"Aye, she could." Mereg chuckled, making notations in a ledger as Cinrak chose from the crates. "But Lyola ain't on these ships. This here is our domain. An' if she don't like the way we work, then she ain't getting any o' the spoils."

Cinrak planted her rearpaws against the slight at-rest roll of the boat. The planks felt more solid to her than land, though they'd only been acquainted for a short time.

"This is not what I've been taught about piratry."

"Some folks be havin' strange notions about us. Can be a headwind into a hurricane, lass." Something deeper than the ocean settled in the dark pool of Mereg's eye. They blinked it away with a smile as wicked as the rapier strapped to their hip. "Ye sure ye not from another boat? Not one of them spies from the anti-unionists, eh? Wouldn't put it past them to try evil on someone so young."

"Yes. I mean, no. I mean, yes, never been on a ship. No, I wouldn't know how to be a spy, let alone a pirate. Why do you ask?"

Mereg raised then lowered her whiskery nose as she gestured Cinrak to lead the way up the stairs. "Fer a first timer on a ship, yer doing ackseptshunally well. Tell ye what, lass. Ye keep that seven percent fer yerself."

Cinrak's hackles bristled. "Whatever for?"

"Settle yer fur." Mereg patted the air. "I jus' saying ye ken yer stuff. Crew always trips down these hold ladders first time." Mereg gestured rearpawwards as they headed up. "An' ye know ye way round them books, theology an' nowt. I see ye got yer eye on that one o' human tales. Not many cabin kits ken haggle e'en in their first star-turns. That deserves acknowledgement. How many star-turns ye have on ye?"

Cinrak blinked in the sunlight and raised her blunt snout. "Sixteen."

Mereg laughed. "Good eye, but not a very good tongue fer lies."

Cinrak sniffed. "Fourteen."

"Better. On the young side, but we seen younger here onboard."

"What d'ya mean by—"

Cinrak swung her face ocean side, eyes narrowing until the bay became a silver-blue blur in her vision.

A sly smile twitched Mereg's scar. "What it be, lass?"

"Wind coming," Cinrak said. "Not till after dark. You'll be wanting to loosen the rope...thingie...there, tighten at that end. Lash down that...thingie...there."

"Ya mean to make sure our good girl here don't turn an' bash the dock. An' there's no fancy word for the wheel." Mereg sniffed the air and nodded. "Ye can smell it, aye?"

Cinrak shrugged. "Can always tell the tides and weather change without looking. What does that mean?"

Mereg's teeth flashed sharp and shining. Even with their good eye closed, it seemed like they could see everything. "Got that pirate salt in yer blood."

A shiver danced down Cinrak's spine.

Stammering her thanks and regards to Mereg's captain, Cinrak barely remembered to breathe as she pounded down the gangway and back to the safety of home.

CINRAK EMBRACED THE OAK as it gave her a protective cloak of shadow.

I wanna jive in a tree too [N]

"You've been a good vessel," she murmured into its trunk. "Stay strong and sturdy for the next kit who needs you."

The lowest branches seemed to curl in around her. The predicted wind-storm or whimsy?

Helet was hosting the tri-tide orphanages' meeting in the front parlour. A neighbour was watching the still sickly Marilette, and the other three kits, all much younger and cuter, sang and recited poems to entertain the committee members. Cinrak had promised to study to get out of the party.

There would be no night like now.

If she started thinking about it, she never would stop, the star-turns would pass and she would be an old maid under Helet's paw, looking after kits for the rest of her suns.

The back gate did her a favour by not creaking as she crept out. *ooh, vibrant moon?*

The Paper Moon fluttered nervously behind scraps of clouds as Cinrak followed the back alleyways. She felt very pirate-ish with her duffle slung over her shoulder and a long red feather she liked to imagine once belonged to a phoenix poked into her hat.

the imagination of youth.. :)

Her eyes grew unexpectedly damp as she neared the docks. She just *had* to touch her favourite city places goodbye: the lower market where she and her friends had spent hours making up stories about the people; the Theatre Rat-oyal, where she used to sit on the fire escape to listen to the operas and plays Helet refused to take her to; and the sewer access door where she used to play ghosts and krakens. ᵇᵒʷˡ

She wiped her eyes clear. Must stay alert for those pirate spies Mereg alluded to! They wouldn't say such a thing unless they trusted her with the secret.

Cinrak paused under the market arch, chewing her underbite, sniffing for trouble. Hmmh. The air tasted normal, except for the increasing wind. This salt thing was unpredictable. *Come on, the oceans inside mammals, speak to me!*

A paunchy porcupine held watch at the *Cry Havoc*. The docks were darker than Cinrak expected. What to do, where to go? Should she wait, or sneak aboard? No, Mereg had preached honesty.

The tavern. Mereg had kept their thirsty gaze on it, watching crewmates with big mugs of cider. A wombat and beaver lounging outside had followed their progress all squidge-eyed. Still, if Mereg went there, it couldn't be all bad.

Having chased everyone inside for the night, the wind whistled around Cinrak's head like a warning horn. The windows were thick with smoky grime. She could discern only shape and shadow.

Cinrak took a deep breath and pushed open the tavern door.

A mug flew passed her face, trailing foam. Raucous laughter broke along with someone's nose. Someone sawed badly on a fiddle, backed up by the off-beat honk of a pipe. A green fairy danced on the wide mantle. Groups huddled over dice and furtive conversations in a variety of tongues. Bowls of soup and stew on the waiter's tray looked thick and dreadful.

It was all Cinrak had imagined a pirate's enclave to be, and more.

With a casual forepaw in pocket grasping her few coins, Cinrak slipped through the crowd.

Don't hold gazes too long. A smile? Yes. No. Not too bright or childish. Try a half smile. A smirk. Yes. Like that ferret over there. Ah, that fit her face well.

A large wooden bar went from end to end of the long room, held up by sailors rolling like they were still upon the ocean.

"Yer too young for ya liquor," the honey badger bartender said before Cinrak had a chance to speak. She pulled hard on an ale handle and malt frothed into an enormous glass.

"Sarsaparilla then, and a tip for some information, if y...ya please," Cinrak said.

"Ooh, we have lady muck in this here place," Honey Badger snorted. Nearby shore rats chuckled. "What can I doo fer yooou?"

Cinrak slapped a coin on the bar and pocketed her shaking paw. "I'm lookin' for Trader Mereg. We have...an appointment."

Honey Badger bit the coin, nodded her satisfaction, and poured Cinrak's inky drink. "Trader Mereg, is it now? Ha. And an appointment, eh?"

Honey Badger winked at the rats. Cinrak took a step to her left and bumped into a belching beaver. She stepped back, but now there was a hustle of squirrels and chipmunks pushing forward for refills.

Honey Badger held Cinrak's glass just out of reach. "I could tell ya where Mereg is, but then I'd expect something a wee extra outta ya."

"But I gave you a tip!"

The rats guffawed.

"In this bidniz, girly, sometimes money ain't effrythin'," said one of the rats, scraping his stool closer. "Bidniz with Mereg ain't undertaken lightly."

This was the pirate life! The salt flying left and right! Just like an adventure from her books. Time to put into practise what she learned from them.

"My b...bidniz with Mereg is none of yours!"

A chorus of 'Ooh!'.

"Listen to this here queen o' the fur," snorted Honey Badger.

Paws clamped on Cinrak's shoulders.

"We all have bidniz with Mereg, whether they likes it or nay," someone growled in her ear.

Before Cinrak could yell, a fist stuffed into her stomach and her back paws left the ground.

A dark maw swallowed her whole into a dank hallway. Head spinning, Cinrak lost all sense of direction.

A gritty floor accepted her face dispassionately. No sound of protest or fight followed. It had all happened so swiftly, obscured by the roil in the main tavern.

She was, desperately and suddenly, rather alone.

A different kind of alone. Not she and the oak, sailing the sky blue. Not she and a book, tripping the imagination wild. Not even alone in a crowd, learning faces, trying on clothes in her mind she could never afford.

Alone with bared teeth, bared knives, and bared souls.

A candle loomed close. Cinrak yelped as the scent of singed fur wafted from her cheek.

"A'ight, girly," said Honey Badger so sweetly. "I recognize ye now. Yer one of Helet's. She been known to associminate with the odd pirate. An' now she pretendin' she all retired from that travellin'. So spit it. Which ships be turnin' coat an' who at court support them irritations?"

"Irate," growled the rat with the knife-like front teeth. "Them all bein' irate."

"Same difference. Well? Don't be coy with us, decoy. If ye be treatin' with Mereg, then yer irate too."

Helet working with pirates? It didn't make sense! "I...I'm capybara. It takes a bit to make me upset."

The room rustled with ugly laughter.

"Ooh, she a funny one," slurred the beaver.

Words were flung at Cinrak's head and she could find nothing on the floor worthy to throw back. Was she sent to stir up trouble? Was Lyola irate? Were those tree-hugging ogres in on it? Them puffer fish kissing mers?

All this talk about upset people and ships. Confusion roiled with the heat and stench in the room. This posse was playing it big, but Cinrak could smell their fear. Was that her salty magic at work?

"I know nothing of what you're talking about. I only came to...I'm a new recruit on the *Cry Havoc*, that's all, I swear!"

Another little lie shouldn't have hurt, but the moment the words left her mouth Cinrak remembered the First Rule: Honesty. Pirates were trained to spot falsehood.

The rabble growled. How many were there? With the candle and the dull shape of the door the only light sources, it was hard to tell.

"She be playing coy," snarled Toothy Rat, a knife appearing in his forepaw. "Let me have some fun. Send a nice warm message to Mereg. That'll get them talkin'."

The fizzle in Cinrak's belly drained away, leaving her stiff and cold. The fear pressure in her head squeezed away all ideas of fight or escape. How would she fight, anyway? Her entire experience had been with stick-swords and lines from "The Fancy Pirate" operetta.

Only one thought remained: she was a fool to think she could be a real pirate.

"'From whose perspective is the truth?'" Quoting the Great Capybara Mother again. "How can I tell the truth when I don't know anything?"

[handwritten: Paladin energy]

Honey Badger and Toothy Rat crowded in as Drunk Beaver held her arms.

Shadows splintered apart with the singing of glass.

The candle went out

The shing-sheen of steel upon steel. A few quick, wet thumps. The sting-scent of iron and salt.

Cinrak slipped as she scrambled backwards. *Blood.* There was blood on the floor. *[handwritten: Brok...]*

"I yield!" shrieked Honey Badger.

Groans from the shore rats.

"I told ye to leave me people alone!"

Mereg's voice.

"I sorry, Cap'n, I sorry." Toothy Rat blubbered.

"This ain't a war, ya cretins," Mereg growled. "Ya want to talk to me, then just talk. Threatnin' mah young 'uns is low. We be pirates. We workin' to be better than our elders. If ye dun want any of that, then ye not be pirates."

A soft paw took Cinrak's shoulder and led her out of the darkness.

MEREG DIDN'T SHEATH THEIR rapier until they were in a quiet back alley. The wind breathed a sigh of relief.

What had been clear and bright and adventure only moments ago slapped Cinrak upside the head hard as a big wave. What if Mereg hadn't known her silly mind? What if they'd been too late? *bro..*

Her legs turned to jellyfish and her large rump hit the cobbles. One of her boots had a spot of blood on it, and she tried to clean it away with spit on claw. "Th-thank you."

"It what I have to do these suns."

Mereg passed back her duffle. Cinrak's belongings were mussed but only her money was missing.

"Did they...call you captain?"

"Aye. Cap'n Mereg the Sharp, o' the IRATE vessel *Cry Havoc*, at yer service."

They shook pirate-style, meeting anew. Mereg patted Cinrak's shaking forepaw, parental-like.

"But..."

"I like to get the way o' the winds in town as soon as we dock. Give the girls a chance to see their families an' a bit o' fun, so I take first watch."

Cinrak took a deep breath, then another. Her brain felt too big for her skull, all squished with new things... and how close she had come to being hurt.

Mereg helped Cinrak stand and tucked her paw into their elbow, like two friends strolling home after a night on the town. "What in all Ratdom possessed ye to go into The Bloody Mary?"

"Ye...you kept looking that way yestersun, and I thought—"

"—ye thought that's where I wanted ta water or had bizniss," Mereg sighed. "Yer an observant soul."

"Yes, captain. Keeps me outta trouble. Usually."

"Hmm. You'd have to be, if yer Helet's kit, aye."

"You do know her! The other pirates said as much. Why didn't you say before? Hey...where are we going?"

"I be taking ye back home."

Cinrak pulled on her paw, but Mereg held her strong, forging through the tragically familiar lanes, saying nothing the rest of the way.

The courtyard gate betrayed them with a creak; the wind had forged ahead with the gossip. The oak cowered as Helet burst from the kitchen, shouting.

The ground's pull turned up and Cinrak's heart tumbled down.

Once Helet ran out of steam—quickly because *what would the neighbours think*—she bundled them into the kitchen and brewed a fresh pot of tea because *manners*. All through the tea ritual, Helet would not look at Mereg, because *Helet*.

"Been a long time, Helet."

The matron set the cups on the table just so. "Not long enough."

"Like that, aye?"

"I told you I was done with all that."

Done with what? Cinrak looked between the two, tongue and throat and stomach so tight she couldn't swallow her tea.

"An' I said ye had a one with salt in her."

She'd met Mereg before? It must've been when she was very young, when Helet still dealt with the pirates in the market.

Back and forth they went, speaking in Adult: icy with disappointment, melting with disdain, refreezing into silence. It was all such an inefficient energy exchange, one Cinrak was determined to remedy when she was grown up.

But why wait? Helet and Mereg were talking about her as if she wasn't there—how stupid she was, nay, how clever—and things *hurt*. Her backside, her stomach, her pride.

A pound of fists and rattle of teacups. Helet performed startlement. Mereg smirked.

"I'm right here! This is about me. Not...whatever you two are still bickering over star-turns later!"

"Disturbin' fairies," Mereg muttered into their teacup.

"Lack of faith," Helet muttered back.

"You're both acting like you're in charge of my life. But you're not. I am! All my friends are gone to whatever pleases them, why can't I?"

"Who's going to help me run the orphanage and start my library for the Great Mother?" Helet wibbled.

"I want to be a pirate. See the world. Meet people. Have adventures. I'm old enough to apprentice. Old enough to choose an academy. I'm old enough to choose to be a pirate."

"Adventure! Pah!" Helet curled her lip. "Disregard for property and life. All these mutterings lately, ship against ship, friend against friend. You'll bring civil war down on us all!"

Mereg scratched the bridge of their nose. "The last time pirates went to war was before my time. Looting and pillaging? Please. A thing o' the past. Our current intership troubles are not without warrant. We're trying to make change for good —"

"Yes, yes, the IRATE." Helet waved the name away. "Pirates and unions. Ha! Go together like a fish and a hook."

"Proper trade, through proper channels, has brought you those books about the Mother. Not that black market extortion and fakes!"

"Wait on," Cinrak demanded. "IRATE isn't some piratey stoush, it's the name of a union?"

Helet's eyes went so narrow they could cut a pumpkin, but Mereg held that gaze without flinching. "Stands for International Rodent Aquatic Trade Entente. The dream o' my old mentor, Wautseaster the Fierce. She said the world be a lot bigger than you can imagine, an' we have to be ready to face any an' everything."

Cinrak swallowed a gasp. The legendary Wautseaster the Fierce had lead the War of the Felidae

Isles to the uneasy truce that stood to this sun. She had disappeared long ago. Her old crew didn't even know what had happened, preferring to spread the rumour she died in a glorious shark riding accident.

"I've heard enough. It's well past your bedtime, young lady—"

"Captain. You showed me a taste of a life I've been dreaming about, and then you snatch it away? Why would you deny someone with my obvious talent?" Cinrak punctuated her argument with quick thumps of the table. The cups murmured agreement into their saucers.

"I didn't say I were bringin' you home," Mereg said, steady as a rock. I jus wanted to show ye how to run away to sea *properly*."

"Eh?"

"First rule o' the ship."

Oh.

"Honesty. Uh. Alright then. Helet." Cinrak sat up as straight as her sore back allowed. "I want to—"

Mereg tilted their head, brow scrunched. Helet's mouth pinched like she'd put too much lemon in her tea.

" —no? I'm *telling* you I'm joining Captain Mereg's crew as...as..."

"My new cabin kit." Mereg's whiskers twitched as if the terrific thought had just transpired

"I'm going to be a cabin kit." Cinrak's eyes glazed as the dream washed over her anew.

A slosh of something passed from Mereg's hip flask to her tea. "An' the second rule o' the ship."

Cinrak scratched her nose. Exhaustion was creeping in on mouse paws. "Loyalty to the crew. Captain, how long is a cabin kit's apprenticeship?"

"Three star-turns. Two if they be very good."

"But that's so long!" Helet wailed, trying out the waterworks this time.

"Pssht. We be back at dock every few tri-tides."

"Two star-turns. If it doesn't work out, if I don't like it...can't imagine how I wouldn't...I'll come back to Ratholme in two star-turns and try something else."

"How will I ever cope with the orphanage without you?" Helet pressed a forepaw to her big chest.

"Pssht." Mereg snorted into their tea again. "The orphanage committee always be there for ye. That what it be designed for."

Helet sniffed.

Cinrak's ears twitched forward, silence her only argument.

Helet sighed. "Fine. Two star-turns. But I want you back for next Aestivus equinox and the running of the stars. You know how much you love that race."

"Wouldn't miss it fer me life," Mereg said, knocking back the last of their tea. "It be a pirate's favourite time o' star-turn!"

A suspicion tickled around the edge of Cinrak's freshly born anticipation for the morning. Mereg knew how this would go all along, the scoundrel!

The agreement was bound between captain and kit with a firm grip of wrists, though Helet insisted she shake social style, paw damp and limp.

"Stay one more night in your home." Helet didn't plead. It wasn't within the realm of the Great Capybara Mother's teaching. "It's late, and I don't want you wandering the streets in the dark."

Cinrak tried to protest but the shake of Mereg's head suggested she'd won enough fights for the night.

"Alright." A good night's rest for her bruised back before she discovered the joys of a ship's bunk sounded quite nice.

"Good. And we can pack for you properly in the morning. That shirt and pants? Tsk. Not nearly good enough for pirate work."

Mereg's voice floated back through the kitchen door, punctuated by the snap of their black boots and whip of long tail. Such stealth! Cinrak hadn't seen them move. "Two star-turns. Ye got yer work cut out for ye, young 'un!"

As Cinrak slept, the oak conspired with the clouds to dapple her dark amber fur with starlight. 🐀

PERFIDY AT THE FELIDAE ISLES

Tail the Second:
In Which Our Newly Minted Capybara Captain Must Deal With a Portentious Prophecy, Mean Schemes, and Cats UH OH.

"**M**URRDERRRR."

"Loqui. Yer talkin' in yer sleep. Again."

"Foul murrrrderrrrrrrr."

"Not me. It you, Cinny."

A tap-tap-tap at Cinrak's cabin window. With a *Loquolchi – Marmot* curse worthy of the marmot diva of the Theatre Rat-oyal, Loquolchi fumbled for a wig pin, while the capybara captain fought with the quilt. *Wot happened* *Timeskip??*

Tap tappity. "Murrderrr —" A hacking cough. "Hurry it up, Cinny. I'm dyin' out here. Lit'rlly."

Cinrak flung open the window and a bird with magnificent fire-russet plumage tumbled onto her desk. The scent of singed feathers filled the room. Cinrak batted the sparks curling the edges of her maps.

31

Loquolchi tipped out a crate of assorted weapons and shoved it under the bird.

"Muriel. What be all this about murder?" Cinrak hiss-whispered. Night still had a firm grip on the good pirate ship the *Impolite Fortune*.

"Good to see ya too, Cinny ya scoundrel. A Cap'n now, no less. Congrabumalations." The phoenix's claws left charcoal stains. "An' Loquolchi too. Just as I saw." Muriel-phoenix

"Me in a prophecy?" Loquolchi preened the black fur around her ears.

Muriel swayed, black eyes hardening with the pressure of the oncoming prophecy. Her voice dropped low. "Yesss, there be murder a-comin'. Things torn apart. Watch the teeth 'n fur. They comes from behin...oh bu—"

Qmfy

The bird collapsed into a pile of steaming ashes.

The capybara captain and her marmot lover stared at the remains of the phoenix for a moment.

"Menopause ain't treating Muriel well." Cinrak fetched the brush and pan.

"How does a bird go through menopause anyway," said Loquolchi, standing cross armed in her flannel nighty. "Not evolutionar-re-rarily possible."

"Phoenixes not be born from eggs, m'love. What came first? The phoenix or the flame?" dwar...

Loquolchi gagged as she picked the last bit of ash from between floorboards. "This puts a dent in re-treating with the Felidae. Murder? Do you think she means an assassination at the treaty talks?"

Cinrak's stomach rumbled at the roast chicken *a h no!*
scent. "We wait 'til Muriel pulls herself together."

So much for their pleasant first cruise together. Her
first major act as a captain had suddenly become a far
harder job that she thought it would be.

Everyone had warned her.

Beware the cats.

THE *IMPOLITE FORTUNE* SAT at anchor just off the main
Felidae archipelago isle. The sun polished the silver
linings of the clouds as an emergency meeting
convened over breakfast in Cinrak's cabin.

Captain Mereg the Sharp, they of the knife-
like silver eye scar, long tail, and longer reach, had
ferried over from their new ship, the *Havoc's Revenge*.
Preferring to work in secret as the head of the IRATE
union, especially with the relationship between crown
and pirates still tender, Mereg presented that morning
as Cinrak's friend and mentor.

Queen Orvillia, a handsome rat with black and
white fur, made a prim and furtive entrance. Columbia,
the mer ambassador with red hair, beard, and scaled
tail, swam in fast from the main Felidae lagoon.

Loquolchi took it as her specific duty to guard
Muriel's ashes. She gave anyone outside the cabin the
evil eye. Cinrak could almost see the thoughts wisping
out her ears, like rage smoke: *Are you the murderer? Are
you?* Cinrak had to softly remind her they were all her
crew, and all her friends.

Everyone kneeled to the queen as she entered.

"Oh, get up you lot," Orvillia said, making irritated circles with her forepaws. "You're embarrassing me. Ohh, is that brie and figs? Don't mind if I do. So, how long until Muriel reconstitutes?"

"Anything a'tween a couple or a dozen turns of the sand glass."

More than a lack of stools kept Cinrak on her paws. Normally the Morning Waft of Warm Welcome from the wind this far north would be most enjoyable, but something sour kept drawing her towards the window. Her nostrils flared and hackles lifted. A strong twinge at her salty weather sense considering the calmness, pleasant heat shimmer, shot through with dancing dolphins, and plucked strings of sunlight.

As he primly nibbled caramel toast, Columbia explained to the Queen that while Muriel's prophecies were Mostly Accurate, they could be interpreted in many ways. Orvillia gave the mer the full force of her attention, large eyes blinking in careful acknowledgement, her tuxedo fur soft, shining, and well groomed even this early in the sun.

A coruscation of concern competed for space in Cinrak's mind. Sun Blasted Sand! She had never been this close to the queen. So *handsome*, with that long tail black as a good night.

She did not need the extra complications of *feelings*. She'd only just found even keel with Loqui after a wild ride of a comedy of manners and stolen kisses behind the Theatre Rat-oyal.

She needed to be the best captain she could be, needed all her attention for these treaty negotiations. Because: *cats*.

Cinrak had to push her annoying, squiddly feelings to the side and decide how much could she trust this new queen. A single head of state or an organization tended to have too many paws in too many power pies. That's why piratry, and now the new IRATE union, always felt like home to Cinrak. Shared responsibility meant shared accountability.

"These discussions with the Felidae are very delicate. It's taken many star-turns to get all parties into a comfortable position. Queen Lyola's ailuro- *wut* phobia, and non-rat rodentphobia in general, left relations between species in quite the messy state." Orvillia sniffed the teapot and poured herself a cup. "The arrival of the phoenix mucks things up. My reign is young and I don't want to leave anything to chance."

Orvillia took whisker tests anew of all the treaty participants. "One of the Felidae ambassadors, perhaps? No, not the ogre mediators; they were early adopters of the idea, and they've shown nothing but kindness to rodentkind. What about IRATE pot stirrers, Captain Mereg? Does your union head have them under control?"

"The agreement a'tween court an' union be paws off, *yer majesty*." Mereg's forepaw strayed towards their sword hip. They satisfied the itch-tell by shoving it in their pocket. "An' aye, Sterickus would know. All union ships are regularly thoroughly vetted."

"And what about the avowed non-union ships?" Orvillia asked, too sweetly.

"Our ears are to the reefs. Nothing gets past my scouts," Columbia assured the queen. He wound one end of his long curly mustache about a finger. She didn't bend that way, but Columbia was the prettiest mer Cinrak knew. He always made Cinrak want to aspire to greater dapper heights. "It's all under control, darling. We've had the Felidae isles staked out for weeks, taking especial care with the undeclared ships. We won't miss a thing with the local dolphins being such chatterboxes!"

The argument went around the table. Loquolchi defended the intel that came through her dressing room from court. Columbia defended the integrity of the Felidae intermediary Rozozau and the grand Clowder; things had changed in the last one hundred star-turns, the cats were proving they could choose nurture over base nature.

All the while, the soft warm breeze made Cinrak's long front teeth ache like a hurricane was blowing.

"An' then there's you," Cinrak levelled her amyg-daliform gaze at the queen.

"Cinny!" Loquolchi whisper-hissed. "I'm sorry, my queen. The captain does not mean that. She knows how beloved you are, that you and I have been friends for a long time."

Orvillia held Cinrak's stare longer than was comfortable.

Her mouth curved into a smile as blunt as her front teeth. "I knew I'd like you, Captain. You embody the best of the first rule of piratry."

"But, your majesty—" Loquolchi protested.

"Whatever happened to your calling me Orvy? And beloved? Pfft. Please. I'm not so enamoured with nice robes and fairy attendants to forget I'll always have enemies. Lyola did not give up her throne gracefully. Captain Cinrak is right to question me. We have to stay sharp."

Mereg chuckle-coughed into a closed fist. Columbia wiggled his bushy eyebrows.

The pressure in Cinrak's broad chest and skull eased only a little. "Thank you, yer maj...Orvy. I be glad ye understand me concerns. The rat and mouse population had the most to fear from the Felidae in the past, an' I'm sure ye—"

A pop, a puff of ash.

"—gger. Murrr...oh, good sun Orvy. Fancy seeing you here."

Hopping on the edge of the crate, Muriel shook her plumage to its full glory of sizzling red, sunset orange, and hot blue-green.

"Muriel." Orvillia bobbed a nod. "Nice to see you again."

"Oof. That was a hard 'un. Came on fast. The Change is unpredictable. Never know when a hot flash gonna trigger me off."

"Funny, coming from a phoenix," Loquolchi said.

"Nothin' funny about it, young 'un." Muriel tilted her head, the gesture the version of a phoenix's grin. "You'll be comin' to me for advice. I know."

Loquolchi choked on a swallow of tea. Her first personal prophecy!

"Apologies for being so forward, but time is short." Orvillia looked poised and regal even in plain blouse and pants. "Negotiations begin tomorrow. The welcoming party is tonight. What do you see?"

"Fur," Muriel intoned, onyx eyes glazing. "Lots of fur flying. Flames. And blood. Water all around."

"Well that be helpful considerin' we be on an ocean." Mereg pulled a blade from one of the many only Cinrak knew they secreted upon their body and began sharpening it.

Muriel continued, "Four will enter, but only three will leave."

"Leave where?" Cinrak prompted.

"A place full of dark and ash," Muriel moaned. "A place under their paws. But the light will come from within and below. And then...*warrrrrrr*."

"Charming," sighed Loquolchi. "People have no taste during war. It's all boring fabrics and ridiculous pantomimes."

"Simple ideas like fear, anger, and hate are easy to control." Orvillia knitted her claws together, shrewdness sharpening her expression to match Mereg's knife. "Someone wants to keep status quo, hide the idea that our history with the cats is far more complicated than eat-or-be-eaten."

Cinrak watched emotions cascade across Loquolchi's sweet marmoty face. Her love was doing the best she could not to let her own history with the Felidae interfere. Her parents had left her an orphan as she'd entered her theatre apprenticeship, venturing on a careless voyage into Felidae lands without a permission or an escort.

The group pressed Muriel for details, and she did her best to describe shape, shadows, the depth of the dark, smells. It could be any ship in the fleet, any basement in the Felidae main island. It could be any four participants, though one had a 'spiky, warm' feel to them. A porcupine assassin? A breakaway from the Ferret Corp?

Cinrak frowned at the warm morning breeze that brought the fragrances of palm and tropical flowers across the lagoon. Mereg squinted their single eye at her, a wealth of worry in their scarred visage. Cinrak gave a little head shake. *Later.*

"Whatever happens, they don't know we have the jump on them," Orvillia said.

Muriel held out a wing, and they slapped paw-feathers.

WARM BREEZE, FLUTTERING FLAGS, kits of all species splashing in the surf. Muriel's bucket dangling from a paw, Cinrak stared down the main Felidae beach, dreaming of a soak in one of hot pools being dug in the sand near old volcanic outflow.

"Wind got your tail?" purred a voice from behind.

Cinrak spun, peering into the thick vegetation, heart pounding. "Peeing Sea Cucumbers! Rozo! What have I told ye 'bout sneakin 'up on me?"

The ginger-pelt cat that oozed out of the bushes only came up to Cinrak's shoulder but he seemed to fill the whole world with his toothy, whiskery grin. "Apologies, still working on breaking that habit."

"Work harder," Cinrak grumbled.

Finding a comfortable bench, Cinrak carefully put down the fancy bucket full of warm ash. Cinrak loved the shady greenery around the Felidae Clowder building. It helped hide how badly she was doing her job.

"Muriel taking another ash nap?" Rozo nodded at the bucket. Fastidious as the dapper captain, Rozo straightened his black vest. Mutual love of well-tailored suits had ensured a firm friendship from the start.

"Good chance for some fresh air an' a spin round the compound." Cinrak scratched her nose and sneezed. The seductively draped humidity did nothing to alleviate the whine in her salty blood.

"You pirates are as jumpy as the Ferret Corp and meticulous as the mer." Rozo put a gentle forepaw on Cinrak's shoulder, claws sheathed. "Relax, Captain. It's under control. No one has ever managed to breach the Clowder, not even in war."

His smile, a dropping of the jaw rather than the spread of lips, was meant to be reassuring, but to a rodent eye it only made him look dangerous. Now who had habits to break?

A yell from the beach. Cinrak fell into a crouch, pulling her hip knife. Rozo's claws flicked out as he sniffed the air.

A combination of pirate and cat crews struggled with a tall tent pole for that night's beach party. Breathing a sigh of relief, Cinrak sheathed her hip knife, Rozo his claws.

"Breathe, captain." Rozo's green gold eyes glowed in the shade. "We have something the would-be assassins don't."

Whiff-pop.

"Me." Muriel clutched the edge of the bucket and cocked her head at a right angle, her biggest, quirkiest 'smile.' She groomed her tail in Cinrak's general direction. "Did I miss anything'?"

"Loquolchi charmin' concessions out o' the Clowder arts council. She an' Queen Orvillia are quite the power team."

Muriel chuckled. "She be a diva a'ight, Cap'n. That fuzzy head she put on in polite company be nothin' but tricksy. Mark my words, her dressin' room will be the one everyone flocks to for information and court gossip in the star-turns to come."

"That be a prophecy?" Cinrak pocketed a discarded phoenix feather. Didn't want something of substantial magical properties falling into the wrong paws.

"Nay. Long observational experience."

With Muriel perched on Cinrak's shoulder, the three wandered through the shaded labyrinthian paths around the Clowder. The island was a carefully curated conservatory of tall trees, colourful foliage, waterfalls, pools, and shady nooks. The buildings merged with the greenery, brick caressed by vines, archways of light and tree limb, flowers filtering colour through windows.

Cats, rodents of all species, and ogres wandered the pathways, nodding greetings and tipping hats as they passed. Mer waved from waterfall lounging or temporary beach dugouts surrounded by ferns and palms.

Cinrak was having trouble untangling the cascade of water. Fat drops on waxy green leaves. The tympanic shuffle across rock and pool. The ooze through dirt and trunk, pipes and waste disposal.

What was real, and what was her heightened suspicion?

The three twisted and turned the many pieces of the puzzle, discussing the newest twist: Columbia's discovery of a bitter current, a crossing of cold with warm unusual for this far north. It had brought a confluence of cetaceans into the feeding area. Rozo worried over the historical over-fishing by Felidae of whale habitats, the violent myths this had created, and what this meant for the negotiations with whales.

"Remind me what ye do again?" Muriel asked as Rozo led them up the gentle ramp to the gallery of wispy curtains and ivy woven balustrades overlooking the main debating chamber.

The noise and motion made Cinrak's hackles twitch. The talks had broken for afternoon tea. Mereg and Orvillia started shouldering towards them from different sides of the chamber.

"I'm a cat of all trades." Rozo slipped easily through the crowd. The cat trusted his land sense as much as Cinrak trusted her ocean.

"He be a spy," Cinrak said out the corner of her mouth just as Mereg slipped into the conversation.

"I'm a *fixer* on international relations," Rozo insisted, grooming his whiskers with forepaws.

"Ye haven't told yer council I not be who I say I be?" Mereg murmured, clapping a forepaw on his shoulder. They had to reach up to do so.

"Your secret is safe with me, your Sharpness."

Mereg flicked their head at Muriel shuffling on Cinrak's shoulder. "How yer feelin'? Any news from the other side o' the veil?"

"Ack. Stupid hot flashes. Come without warning. Interruptin' me flow. Just when I think I can *see* them varmints in me far-seein', I go all—" she threw up her wings. "Whoof!"

A prickle caught the back of Cinrak's neck and she swatted her hackles. Not an insect. She did a long, slow sweep of the chambers calmly lit with filtered sunlight. No one made strange moves. She didn't want to bring the Aspects — the international magic security force made up of the Fairy Council, the Ferret Corp, and Felidae Theurgists — in on the problem. If magic was involved, there could be infiltrators there, too.

"Oh squiddies, she seen me."

Queen Orvillia detached herself from a crowd eager to make her acquaintance. She *glided* in a froofy dress of white, black, and silver that made it difficult to tell where the material stopped and her fur started. She shone with a light of deep night and star's intent.

Oh dear, thought Cinrak. She'd fallen fast and hard.

"A'int ye part o' the next session?"

The queen brushed responsibility away like a fly. "Shipping rights with the ogres and whales. I'm not needed."

Rozo glanced over the balustrade at the ogre contingent making themselves comfortable across the table from the Clowder. Cinrak noted how his eyes flicked around the room. "But I am. If you'll excuse me?"

He bowed out of their presence.

"Shall we?" Orvillia gestured towards an exit.

"But —"

Orvillia cut Cinrak a *look*. "*Shall* we?"

The Queen scythed a swathe through milling cats, smile-and-nod practised and easy.

So many cats. Ginger, calico, white, black, black and white, silver, tabby, beige, brown, and blue. Green-gold and blue eyes watching them furtively, hundreds of star-turns of unrest, evolution, and learned self-control sitting awkwardly between rodent and feline.

"Who's a pretty birdy, then?" asked a fluffy white matron in parrot-speak.

"*I* be, thank you for noticing," Muriel preened.

The cat scurried away, ears twitching.

"Where's Loqui?" Cinrak asked, fumbling for small talk.

She was surprised to see the queen's blush. "Changing her wig, I presume. She seems to have one for every occasion."

"Goes well with her opinions on all things art."

Cinrak covered her grin by admiring a bright orange flower. Loquolchi's hard shell, designed by trauma and hardened by court life, shielded a soft touch and an open heart. They shared good taste in women!

After having Mereg check the area, Orvillia guided them into a shady spot with an embracing palm frond.

"A'ight, what be buggin' ye, yer majesty, Cinrak." Mereg put a forepaw on their sword hip. "Yer both jumpy as piranha."

"It be, err, me instincts." Cinrak widened her eyes in Mereg's direction. The queen didn't know about her salty magic.

"Oh aye?" Mereg's paw tightened on their rapier pommel. They'd been mentor and protégé so long, they immediately grasped her meaning. Cinrak hoped Mereg had done their due diligence with the Aspects and weather mages employed by some IRATE vessels.

"Think a storm be comin'."

"Hmph. That'll put a damper on tonight's festivities," Orvillia said. "Will need to reassess my outfit."

"An' you, yer worshipyness?"

"Me?" Orvillia sat primly twitched the upper layers of her dress to let some air onto her fur. "Cinrak was the one who sent me that messenger squirrel."

"Nay. I been doin' the rounds with Muriel all this time."

"Can confirm." Muriel clutched Cinrak's padded shoulder so tight her claws cut in. "She doin' a great job o' lookin' after me. There with a nice place for me to relax whenever I need an ash nap."

"Not doin' it entirely for altruistic reasons," Cinrak said, touching a waxy leaf, trying to taste the water in the air. It gave her nothing.

"Ye wouldn't be a pirate if ye were." Muriel tilted her head.

Orvillia gave an annoyed grunt. "Enough of the mutual appreciation society. The message. It was in your paw writing, Captain! You said you needed to talk, urgently. About—" Orvillia flicked her head at the phoenix. "—you know what."

Cinrak looked at Mereg. Mereg looked at Orvillia. Orvillia looked at Cinrak. Muriel looked at them all, feathers all fluffed out, pacing up and down Cinrak's outstretched arm in agitation.

"This is not good. Not good. Farting Westerly Winds, is it hot or is it...murrrrderrrr. Oh bugg—"

Whoompf.

Cinrak got the bucket up just in time to catch Muriel collapsing into ashes.

Rapier drawn, Mereg turned a slow circle. Even Orvillia had a knife.

Cinrak's head felt fit to burst, salt scraping wildly at the inside of her skull and bones.

Heat like a dozen tiny knives slid into Cinrak's back, creeping perilously close to the main artery in her neck.

Mereg and Orvillia froze at the same time, whiskers twitching.

"Don't move, friends," a voice whispered. "Or you will bleed out in moments. Put the phoenix down and surrender your blades. Slowly."

A shimmer like heat on water slid all around them, muffling the jungle, cutting off distant voices.

"That's it. Good girl."

Their blades floated away from their paws and disappeared into the shimmer. Orvillia's coal-chip eyes widened. Cinrak tried to communicate her chill across the space between them, but her salt overrode everything, burrowing the marrow out of her bones.

Mereg twitched, going for one of their hidden blades.

"Don't even think of doing anything stupid," hissed the voice. "We won't hesitate to start something in the chamber. Would be awful. Lots of dead. Blood on your paws."

Cinrak took a breath to speak, but the knife-shriek heat in her flesh rose to a scream. Sunshine exploded into slivers of sliver-black sparkles, and a door opened onto night.

MOONFIRE CASCADING ALONG HER spine brought Cinrak to some semblance of consciousness. The dark remained total.

"Well, I not be dead." Cinrak pulled against her bonds. Heat clamped sharp on her wrist, ankles, and waist. "Yer highnessing?"

"How undignified," grumbled Orvillia. "And I told you to call me Orvy."

"Mereg?"

A grunt.

"Muriel?"

A waft of roast chicken scent.

"Where. Are. We?"

"Don't try to get out of yer ropes, yer...Orvy. They be magicked," Cinrak said. As soon as she stopped struggling, the prickly pain ceased. "An' we be on board a ship."

"I can feel that."

Sarcasm. Good. Something to focus on other than being afraid.

"Doesn't smell like the *Impolite Fortune*. Or the *Havoc's Revenge*."

A thunk and another grunt. "Chair bolted to floor. Can't get over there t'gnaw ya free."

"Mereg! I told ye not to move! How ye be?"

"Head hurts. Like a kraken bin playin' whip ball with it."

A lie, but not a lie. Now was not the time to call Mereg on it.

Silence. No pawsteps and voices. A damp shroud like heavy wool held their senses in place.

"Can ye feel anything, Cinrak?" Mereg asked.

Orvillia made a confused noise.

"I be tryin'. But me head hurt like blathery when I push against. Whoever it be, their magic hard 'n fast."

Another confused noise from the queen.

Cinrak sighed. Not the best way to reveal her secret.

"I got that pirate salt, yer...Orvy. Of that special kind. Taste the weather, people's movements, shadows, an' such like."

"Oh. *Oh*. That's...good to know."

Whoops, there's that sarcasm, Cinrak thought.

Orvillia muttered to herself for a moment. "Does that mean...?"

"I felt somethin' comin'. Like Muriel. But whoever they be, they good at it. Apologizin', yer majesty."

"Cinrak." Orvillia's voice softened to something Cinrak could very much learn to love. "Cinny. Stop it. They've broken the rules of engagement. Played sinister tricks. Used outlawed magic, I suspect, if you or the Aspects or Muriel couldn't pick up on it."

The thought she was too young, too inexperienced, for this captain's gig ruffled Cinrak's fur. Was she to blame for their predicament? Had she inadvertently allowed Muriel's vision to come true?

"Muriel?" Mereg grunted.

"In a bucket," Cinrak said.

"Aye? Me ears ringing. Speak up."

"She be snoozin'." Cinrak chewed her thoughts for a moment. "They came for us. Specifi-kicka-lally."

"You mean me." Orvillia sounded like she could cut something into small strips, nice and neat. "Treating with the Felidae was my idea."

"Yer part right, Orvy. I s'pect they wanted Muriel and Mereg. I be a lucky catch."

"Union busters." Mereg sounded terribly pained.

"But why didn't they take Sterickus?"

"Apologizin', yer majesty. I needed to find out if I could trust ye. Uhh—" Cinrak was thoroughly concerned for her mentor. "I be the true head of IRATE. Don't like all them eyes on me. Can't think straight at the table. Sterickus be hard-headed as a porcupine can come, which makes her a better face fer IRATE. I be there just to shuffle papers."

Orvillia made a noise like she was sucking air through her front teeth. "Anyone else have something they should share with me? You know, your *queen*."

Cinrak didn't think it appropriate to share Rozo's job description, even if she wasn't entirely sure what that job was.

"You really are quite tenacious," came a voice out of everywhere and nowhere, part of the night-claws itself. "I would advise against fighting your bonds. That saltiness, as you so eloquently describe it, may just crystallize under too much pressure."

A squeeze upon Cinrak's brain, like barometric pressure had just jumped. She yelped.

The voice continued, "No use trying to figure out who we are. I'm not one of those idiots who spills my plan only to have you escape by dissecting it, or turning us against each other. Just know that there are *many* of us working to stop this sham of a treaty, and you *will* die once you stop being useful."

Silence like a bell toll.

"Wonder what they mean by us bein' useful," Cinrak muttered.

No reply.

"Cap'n?"

No reply.

"Blatherin' Beasties of the Deep."

Pwap!

In the flash of the phoenix's feathers reforming, Cinrak caught a glimpse of her mentor slumped against their bonds, and a very annoyed rat queen.

" —er! They be comin', they usin' the waters! Ooh cripes...this ain't good. No no no! Barnacles, who put the sun in here. Cinny, halp!"

Fwoof.

"Now I'm hungry," Orvillia grumbled.

CINRAK CAME TO LOATHE the sound of her heartbeat. She had no sentiment for the squishy organ, having seen how they worked. And stopped working.

Orvillia passed the time by talking through her memories of disaffected mages and fairies. Hearing her voice laced with sarcasm and silly plans helped Cinrak stay focused on something, anything, even if it was a plan to take the queen *and* Loqui on a night's sail on her captain's sculler.

When they got out of this.

If.

Mereg came and went in decreasing degrees of sensemaking. Cinrak and Orvillia spoke and sang, but nothing kept them awake long.

Muriel popped up twice, but whatever magic bonds held the three from the real world held Muriel back from full encorporeality.

Cinrak tested the edges of their prison with gentle prods of her salt. Magic was magic, and could be undone with magic, she reckoned. After much pain and narrowing her focus, she found a small worn patch in the dark weave beneath her paws. Their captors were not expecting any approach from under water, and the weather seam was clumsily tied off at the base of the oval Cinrak discerned encased the prison.

Despite the flaw, the threads of night were tougher than ship ropes. Gnawing at them with her salt was like unpicking skeins with a single pin. She could manage to snip a pawful before she had to stop and swallow against the bile. Snip, breath, swallow, repeat.

Cinrak muttered dirty shanties to keep the queen chuckling and herself focused.

She may have fallen asleep. The dark made it hard to tell.

Finally. Her salt whittled down to only a few grains, head spinning, she tore a tiny hole in the magic weave.

Cinrak wriggled her senses through, tasting the warmth of the water, listening for its light. They were on the north side of the island and the sun was already despondently descending. With the rest of the Felidae Isles stretched east towards the ogre peninsula, a vessel could scarper west and be quickly lost in the wide expanse of the Unknown.

Ah, but here: a push against what little remained of Cinrak's salty energy. The bitter currents Columbia spoke of. A side effect of the weather manipulation to hide the ship. What had Columbia said? Dolphins and whales were feeding well.

She tried a click-whistle to attract a dolphin, but the prison's bonds snapped the sound to pieces. Cinrak pulled back, spat bile. She was so close to *something*, some new understanding.

The tide was turning. The ocean, too big to influence, every part of it connected to every other part, known and unknown. But she didn't have to reach to the other side of the Unknown. Just the other side of the reef.

Pushing through the tear, Cinrak birthed ripples in the viscosity. The effort almost drowned her senses, whipping away what little remained of her salt, but dammit...more lives were at stake than her own. She could not condone the mistrust and war that could brew up from this one misconstrued moment. One of Orvillia's election planks had been an insistence on overseeing the end to war. She did not want to let her new friend down.

"Mereg," Cinrak barked. "Time to turn tha *Havoc* into tha wind, ye old salty rat!"

Mereg mumbled something that may have been a curse.

"Orvillia, I be needin' yer help. Sing at me so I don't be faintin'."

Mereg mumbled some semblance of notes that sounded like the Shanty of the Kraken and the Whale. Orvillia picked up the response to the call. The surprise at the queen knowing the bawdy tale gave Cinrak the final impetus to push hard, sending a warning ripple out into the ether.

Cinrak's salt gave out at the same time as Mereg's voice and she descended into darkness.

ICY FIRE, WHISPERING.

Scale and teeth. From the depths. Gnawing her bones.

Pop and sizzle of joints. Fireworks attacking the stars for their disinterest, bringing them down to rest against empty eyes.

Iron, creating iron, metal to fluid.

Shouts, harmonizing with the dirty skies of dawn.

VOICES WOVE AROUND CINRAK's head, like the Three Capybara Sisters couldn't decide whether to knit or cut her ties.

"I don't believe in fate," Cinrak murmured, trying to push away insistent paws.

"Cinny, hush, it's alright." Loquolchi's voice emerged from the babble. "You have cuts on your head. No, don't take that off, you woolly headed mammoth!"

Shadows lurked at a sensible distance between Cinrak and her knife paw.

"Ya make a terrible nursemaid," Cinrak grumbled. "Ya think ya dyin' if ye have a cold."

Loquolchi sniffed. "You're welcome. You gave me such a fright. I thought you were dead."

Another face floated into her vision. Orvillia. Even monumentally annoyed she looked strong and handsome to Cinrak.

"You saved us, Cinny. You saved the whole treaty, possibly the world from war."

Cinrak made a rude noise at what she thought about 'saving' the world. "Mereg?"

"Alive, and safe."

Loquolchi answered too quickly.

She didn't like it one bit. Not the being lied to, and definitely not the being seen by her queen wearing some silly nightgown!

"Well done, scamp." Rozo, with Muriel on his shoulder.

Muriel hopped on to the blankets and nuzzled Cinrak's cheek. "I'll be a pterodactyl's uncle if you didn't help divert a prophecy."

"Pterodactyl nothing." Cinrak made another rude noise, enjoying the caress.

"Don't make fun, Cinrak," Muriel scolded. "It's no small thing to fight the strings of time and space and win. The stars are looking down on you, I'm sure."

"None of that murder stuff?"

"A few nasty rats and their fairy mages got a little roughed up, but no one suffered anything near a deathly wound," Orvillia explained, laying a soft forepaw on her arm. Near Loquolchi's paw. Two warm, lovely paws on her fur.

Cinrak shoved the pleasant thoughts away. "Mereg."

"I said—" Loquolchi began.

Orvillia sighed and looked away. "They're with Columbia. Who heard you. Columbia, I mean. Alerted everyone. Followed the trail. The Aspects tore apart the illusion and a strike team of IRATE pirates over-powered the terrorists' vessel."

Icy water raced through Cinrak's veins followed by flying embers. A sign of respect for the watery world they shared, the mer sang for pirates who had been gravely injured. Their song was rumoured to ease the way to a pirate's last voyage, or ease them back from the brink of their wounds.

Cinrak did not know of any pirates who had been sung back.

"Take me to them," Cinrak whispered.

A wheeled chair appeared. Rozo offered Cinrak his velvet jacket, slightly crumpled from the evening's events. She adorned herself gratefully.

The bustle of the cool Clowder buildings parted to make way for the procession. Cinrak hurt too much to take in their stares. And bows. Sweet Squiddies, could the cats stop *bowing*?

Her friends gave her the quick and dirty run down: a collusion of an IRATE splinter group and Felidae factionists had employed rogue fairy weather mages.

The irony was not lost on Cinrak: enemies working together to remain enemies. They would receive a fair trial, which was far more than the terrorists were willing to offer their opponents.

"Invisibility magic." Cinrak spat the poisonous taste of treason. "No wonder me salty blood was pricklin'. Banned fer a reason. Some people just don't like fairness."

The glow of fairies glimmered in the trees and mer scale flashed in the lagoon. The sun pulled the horizon around its shoulders and the ocean whispered a gentle lullaby. A large group of cats and rodents sat along the beach, learning the harmonies to the sweet song coming from a hut on the tide line. Muriel settled atop the hut, glaring at the ocean as if she could keep all tides at bay.

Cinrak tried to adjust a bow tie that wasn't there.

She felt quite furless.

Columbia's sweet baritone faded. He offered Cinrak a sad smile, red beard and hair unkempt.

"Cinrak, you crusty old barnacle," Mereg croaked, blinking their misty eye. There was something ruthless in how small and limp her mentor was lying in Columbia's arms.

Cinrak limped over and sat with a dramatic sigh. "Told ya we'd get outta it."

"Aye."

"We needs a good soak in a mountain spa, methinks."

"Aye."

Cinrak eyeballed Columbia. He gave a lopsided grimace and a half shrug. "They took quite the blow to the head."

"Kraken's Arse, he singin' is keepin' me awake."

"Ah, you grumpy old eel," Columbia grinned. "You love it."

"Tired," Mereg mumbled.

The mer took up humming again, weaving the diagnosis into a tune. "Their balance is affected. They'll never be able to stand upon the ocean again."

"I be right here, ye know."

"And you know all this, my lovely," Columbia crooned.

Cinrak pushed away her feelings again. It was all a bit much. She settled on the bigger picture; an international crisis may have been averted, but the new and fragile IRATE might be in trouble without its best proponent.

"Aye, I can see what's all flashin' through yer head. An' that—" Mereg tapped Cinrak's chest. "—be why I nominate ye take over as head of IRATE."

Cinrak chewed her underbite, a habit she thought long gone with her innocence. "Nay. I be too young."

Mereg grunted, somewhere between pain and amusement. "You'll see I be right come election time. Everyone loves a level-headed an' handsome capybara. Too young? You're smart an' kind. Everyone knows that. Trust yer crew."

That was all Mereg could manage for that sun, and many suns after.

Muriel fell to ash and pulled herself together with effort. Loquolchi leaned on Orvillia's shoulder. Something new and delicate burgeoned there; Cinrak wanted in, though the weight of new responsibilities added extra to her painful back. Rozo's whiskers shivered; his flicking tail spoke of agitation towards his betraying fellows.

The treaty between Felidae and Ratdom was not a done thing yet.

Unable to look her friends and lover in the eye, Cinrak held Mereg's paw and focused on the one thing she knew best. The ocean sighed against the sand, telling the land in broken whispers how to take care of one of its favourite children.

The Wild Ride of the Untamed Stars

Tail the Third:
Where Our Capybara Captain Attempts to Lasso Truth, Love, and Light

S ILENCE HOVERED IN ANTICIPATION over the racers. The Moth Moon caressed the fairy-light-spangled podium with her gentle smile. The Paper Moon peered over the lavender horizon, knowing better than to risk rising on the night of sharp-edged falling stars. And the Silver Moon cut carefully undulating hills with slivers of brightness.

A barrel-chested capybara stepped forward from the petitioner's line. "Cinrak the Dapper, Captain o' the most excellent IRATE ship the *Impolite Fortune*, an' I ride in the Grand Chase of the Falling Stars fer the Queen's Paw."

A most satisfying gasp from the crowd of petitioners, court adjuncts, fairies waltzing the breeze, and rodent rabble.

"A capybara as the rat queen's consort?"

61

"There's a reason they say the sea-farer's union puts the 'IRATE' into pirate!"

"Not since the First Ride..."

Cinrak adjusted her purple bow tie, swinging her broad snout from side to side, trying to hold her grin in check. The court was all a-bluster? Good.

The Rat Queen Orvillia pressed her with her coal-dark eyes. The jewel at the centre of the Queen's crown throbbed, an ache against the festive mood.

This was the bargain they'd discussed, of a sort. Cinrak had promised to petition for the jewellery of Orvillia's well-adorned right forepaw, putting the orphanage of Cinrak's upbringing in the black and IRATE ships bound to pleasure cruises rather than duty for some star-turns to come. But promises were flexible, even to the head of the Independent Rodent's Aquatic Trade Entente.

"Petition—" Orvillia's whiskers twitched. " —accepted."

A crackle-hiss, like lightning along a sword drawn from its scabbard. Cinrak turned her snout up. The stars were close; she could smell their light, fresh as a storm before it hit the sea.

With their attention caught by the busy sky, no one noticed a new petitioner step up until her sweet, high voice pierced the night.

"Loquolchi, Lead Soprano of the Theatre Rat-oyal, and I ride for the Queen's Paw."

Another gasp. A few onlookers took knees.

"You blewdy diva," Cinrak grumbled. "Trust you to upstage everythin'."

Taking her place in line, the marmot graced her pirate lover with a toothy smile. "Can't let you have all the fun, Cinny."

"Petition accepted." Orvillia's smooth politician voice shimmered with amusement and fondness.

"We had a *deal*," Cinrak hissed to Loquolchi as Orvillia swept forward and began reciting the rules of the Ride. "I'm doin' this for *both* o' us, Loqui."

Loquolchi looked off into the darkness like she was steadying herself to deliver a beloved aria. "I love Orvillia, too. Besides, a little competition is *fun*."

There was no stopping the hard-headed diva once she set her course. Cinrak straightened the hem of her tailored suit jacket and eyed Loquolchi's riding garb: a batwing dress straight out of the Rat-oyal costume department, all white froof and flop. Surely a tripping hazard.

Another crack-hiss. Cinrak, accustomed to listening for tiny changes of wind in the rigging, swung her blunt nose up. There. Way high, a tiny pinprick of a star against the bruised velvet sky

Ah! thought Cinrak. *To be only the second rodent in history to capture and ride a falling star!* Fame, riches, and the rat court would be there for Cinrak the Dapper's asking.

Sssssssinraaaaaak...

But tonight, like every other Aestivus equinox, she had watched the stars fall, dance, sizzle, break to rainbow sparks, and climb again, something strange pulled at her heart, tweaking her storm senses.

Ssssinraaaaaaak...

Cinrak was running before Orvillia had finished her recitation of the Grand Chase's thousand star-turns history or Loquolchi could pinch her for luck.

A thunder of paws mixed with the thunder of the falling stars hitting air. Breath huffed. Leather and rope slapped against gloves.

Angling away from the cut of the Silver Moon's smile, Cinrak dug deep into the secret Alice pocket sewn into her jacket. If anyone had been so brazen as to attempt to loot the locked trunk under her billet aboard the *Impolite Fortune*, they would have been surprised by the paw that emerged as if from thin air to grab a red, silky rope. That is, if they hadn't already been surprised to death by the poison kraken-spirit Cinrak had given a home inside the padlock.

Cinrak had scoured the myths and stuck to the letter of the rules; reins were allowed only if they were soft natural materials that wouldn't harm the stars. Mer-hair, made from night brushed a thousand times over into silken tresses, was supposed to soothe the star enough to allow it a passenger. Legend said like spoke to like.

"Illegal buckles!" shouted the magpie referee keeping pace, and another racer, a beaver in a gaudy gold robe, fell away.

Though Cinrak had a good head start, her stubby legs couldn't hold the lead for long. The stars were crackling in earnest.

Ssssssssiiinraaaaaak...

"I see spurs!" screeched the referee. Another participant, this time a squirrel, went down in a flurry of tail.

"Metal harness!" The referee was relishing his job, and a mole rat fell out of the race, muttering darkly about bad luck and nasty, nasty magpies.

The Moth Moon did its best to get out of the way of the rodent runners powering uphill. Decent-sized stars had started to dip low.

There was no use wasting her breath in cajoling and promises. Cinrak tightened her fist on the first loop in her pocket. Still natural material, still legal.

The bottom of the Moth Moon popped free of the hilltop with a satisfied sigh just as Cinrak chose her mark. The biggest and brightest tended to be too tumultuous and broke up into baby stars, the perfect ride to satisfy the ego of those only seeking to impress the queen. Those in the know, the race old-timers, went for a middling-sized star, the ones at the back of the pack, the more circumspect and less like to burn out.

Cinrak drew the plaited rope free. At the sight of mer-hair appearing as if from nowhere, a racing gopher beside Cinrak stumbled in surprise and yelled for a judgment.

"No foul!" squawked the magpie dodging sparks from the air-skittering stars.

A huff of breath on Cinrak's left, a delicious sound: Loquolchi.

A loud and familiar sound: FWUMPH.

With arms spread wide and a sail made of bright Moon Moth silk draped between, Loquolchi swooped overhead in a casually theatric pose like she was born for the sky and took the lead.

"Clever girl!" Cinrak shouted and waved. How had Loqui bribed enough silk out of the recalcitrant insects to catch the beams at perigee?

Cinrak then cursed as Loquolchi beat haste towards the best-looking star. The star pulled back from the rush towards the impossible — the moment of balance between equal light and equal night — to admire the scintillating wings.

A mistake. Loquolchi swung up and over the spiky perch and settled between the star's largest limbs.

With the silky rope tightening in anticipation on its own accord in her paw, Cinrak had to concede First Catch. It meant little if a rider couldn't get the star over the finish line with no harm done to its ephemeral existence. Loquolchi knew the skills of hot air but only what came from within, not without.

In the thousand star-turns of the race's existence, only one star had suffered a rider to the end and crossed the finish line. That star now shone from Orvillia's crown, a warning to its descendants.

Alerted by the fizzing sparks and bucking cracks, other stars dipped to assist their sibling. The pants, growls, and shouts from the rest of the petitioners fell away. Cinrak's attention hove fully to the glimmering prizes pricking the Aestivus sky and dodging the playful Moth Moon. More light meant a longer dance with the shy moths who dotted their cocoons across her craters.

The red rope formed a lasso and sprang out before Cinrak had instructed her muscles and eight digits. She barely had time to lay grip upon the knotted end when the rope pulled taut, having found its mark upon a blue-ish elder star.

Such was the way of mermaid's hair, made to unerringly find and caress the stars.

Despite hard-worked shoulders, Cinrak had never fought a storm such as she fought with this star. Though the star was of the lumbering type, its orneriness almost wrenched her arms from their sockets. With very little breath left, she dashed to keep up, her six toes tripping through then lifting above bramble bushes as the star pulled indignantly away from the excited rabble.

Surely lost! Cinrak kicked at the air, paws slipping further along the mer-hair rope. "To the bottom of the sea wit' ye!" she yelled into the rushing wind and the star's crackle-delight.

Paw over paw, like climbing to the nest in a hurricane, Cinrak fought her way up the rope wriggling with a mer's brushed-in mirth. A lucky break: the star dipped to avoid an onrush of over-excited young stars breaking like fireworks against each other.

Cinrak got a leg over.

The mer-hair rope wrapped neatly around a flashing limb as the star bucked and swayed.

Mer-hair held firm but not brutal.

"It's not like that," Periwinkle had whistled as Cinrak laboriously plaited the rope: a gruelling harvest; many tri-tides of supplication to mer needs, picking abandoned strands from sea-weeded rocks and bone combs. "The myths about our hair are such a farce! Never let the fearful tell your legend, Sssinrak-Dapper."

Stripped of her captain's title and fancy coat, Cinrak had risked her life, loves, IRATE union career, and ship to parlay with the mer-people. Then suffering through salty fur, eating more fish than she cared to entertain, insults, chilblains, and drudgery in the effort to hook herself a star and a heart.

Tonight she would find out if it had all been worth it.

The star whipped upwards, pushing tears from Cinrak's squinted eyes and a scream from her lungs. Wind tore at her best suit, threatening to turn it to tatters. Despite having ridden into countless storms, excitement and fear tossed her about as much as her mount. She clung on for her life as the star tore across the sky, causing even the Moth Moon to hastily back-pedal at their passing.

The star roared — Cinrak thought she could almost hear words in the mess, whipping around its youngers, going up-see-daisy over another rider: Loquolchi, moth wings a-streaming and marmot-melisma shaking sparks from frantically flashing arms.

The will to win struggled hard against Cinrak's will to love. *Loqui be deservin' better'n this. She deservin' Orvillia too. But to be a new light in the crown... Oh, Stars!*

Unusually, four riders now held tenacious grips, the rest a furry ball of limbs and curses on the hillside. A chinchilla courtier screeched as it rode a tight spiral, followed by a spring-hare from a family who sent a race petitioner every star-turn. Neither looked as if they'd keep their mounts for long, the way the young stars bucked.

Loquolchi, however, held fast. Wrapped securely, the silk wings applied double duty, soothing the star as well as helping her keep her seat. She marmot-shrilled somewhere between a frightened scream and perfect high melisma.

And she was pulling ahead.

Cinrak, calling upon all the practise she'd done with the narwhals, bent low and kissed the mer-hair rope. How would it respond this high up? It was a being of the sea, not the air, pulling stars down with mer song to meet with their sibling celestials in the deep, not to tame them. She didn't want to force sup-plication. The stars had travelled too far, shone upon too much, for such brute force.

"Fly, darling star, *fly!*" Cinrak yelled. She didn't kick at the star's sides like others would a beast mount. Stars were too precious for that.

The star leapt ahead like a dolphin racing the *Impolite Fortune*'s bow. Cinrak almost tumbled off the back, only holding her perch by the sheer force of her thick thighs and quickly looped sailor's knot.

Hills spun by, their grass dark as blood in the violet night. Tree heads whipped as they watched the riders pass. They shook their limbs in consternation and delight.

Cinrak grabbed the lead. Then, with a warble, Loquolchi sung her star forward.

The chinchilla and spring-hare couldn't compete. A crash, too fast to see in the strobing starlight, a flail of rodent and star limbs, and then a tumble. The two young stars shot off to rejoin their siblings.

The race looked lost. Cinrak didn't have the promises of beauty and immortality Loquolchi sung to her star. It seemed erratic though, hitching and hurrying. The marmot's voice was strong but couldn't hold out forever in the thinner air.

"What can I give ye, when ye have all the sky at yer disposal?" Cinrak whispered frantically.

The front-most arm of the star flashed the brightest yet. Pointing perhaps? At the finish line. And at the finish line...

A tickle travelled from the mer-hair rope up her arm to the base of her thick neck. The strange songs the mer-people had sung for her about the slow swing of stars started to make sense! Yes! That's it! The stars were precious, but also...*alive*.

Cinrak moved her lips from the mer-hair and buried a single promise into the stark limbs of the star: "I will set yer siblin' free."

The star bucked like a lover and surged ahead, weaving like a dolphin but always coming back dead-on to the target: the flickering crown upon Orvillia's head.

Another thrust of moth-wing in her vision. Loquolchi came neck and neck, shrilling through her drawn-back teeth, her star-mount flashing sparks in time to her song.

One final high note from Loquolchi, and...

There was nothing between them as they sailed over the finish line.

Thighs and biceps trembling, Cinrak's dismount was more fall than finesse. Loquolchi managed to maintain some of her diva flow as the star let her go but only thanks to the products of a moth's bottom. Obligatory cheers and a hish-hush of surprise rippled through whiskers and cupped claws. Not just the second winner in the history of the Great Chase, but a dead heat!

Cinrak grimaced into her now-mutilated bow tie. So many things warred within her pirate soul: love and annoyance for her marmot beau, pride and surliness at the shared win, a tenderness for her star.

Strangely, the two mounts bobbed in place, as if waiting.

Orvillia stepped forward, her crown lighting the way. Cinrak's gaze and canny thoughts moved quickly from queen to waiting star to the light kept captive inside the headpiece by generations of rat queens.

Orvillia paused, watching the prize of Cinrak's face. Her eyes flicked up at the same time she flicked a wicked knife free of her sleeve. Whispering deep, strange words, the queen tapped her right paw to the centre of her crown. The jewel throbbed, silvery light encasing her paw, creating a glove shimmering with the gifts of the sky. Orvillia tapped her wrist with the knife's edge – gently, a ritual only – and the doppleganger paw broke free, leaving its flesh twin behind.

The crowd gasped.

"As petitioned, as promised," Orvillia said, offering the ghost glove to Cinrak. "Will you marry me?"

Cinrak trembled as she bent low over the glimmering prize. She kissed the paw, real and unreal; the latter as solid as the former. "My majesty, nay. I love ye, but the sea is my mistress."

The crowd tittered, and fairy hairdos flashed green and blue in surprise. Relief bent Orvillia's grin into a jaunty angle.

"As for you..."

Orvillia turned to Loquolchi, who perfected her best sweeping bow, the moth dress aflutter. She looked between the capybara and marmot, her gaze dipping for a moment from midnight shrewd to a new-moon ocean delight.

A touch of left paw to the crown, a flick of the knife, and she presented another phantom finery to Loquolchi. "Will *you* marry me?"

Loquolchi pulled upright and brought the spectral spoils to her heart. "By the stars, no! I love you, but the stage *always* comes first!"

Orvillia breathed a sigh of relief. "That's settled then. Marriage is such a ridiculous institution--all silly glances and restrictions on who to take to bed. Those tokens will get you into my court any time. Use them at your will, my loves."

Orvillia planted a kiss on each of their cheeks, one-two, one-two. Blushes flourished. Tense glances offered reconciliation, then Cinrak and Loquolchi buried kisses in each other's furry faces.

The crowd roared. *Two* consorts to the queen? And unmarried? Outrageous! Romantic!

Cinrak's grin almost broke her face in two.

"One more thing, m...my love." Cinrak said.

The queen cast an eyebrow as sharp as her knife.

With her rapier-honed reflexes giving the queen no time to react, Cinrak snatched the crown from Orvillia's brow. The crowd fell into chaos, guards having to be elbowed back by Orvillia.

A swift twist of metal softened by the internal star's breath, and Cinrak snapped the crown in two.

The star flowed out of its prison.

A thrum gripped the hearts of every rodent present. The two star-mounts danced around their freed sibling, bearing it carefully back to its cradle of the long, deep sky. Orvillia muttered a furious incantation, but the star ignored her, racing upwards. She heaved a sigh, shrugged, and offered Cinrak a smile equal parts shrewd and conciliatory. Oh aye, Cinrak knew she had a wily one on her paws here!

Loquolchi fiddled with the two pieces of the crown trying to fit them back together.

Cinrak put her arms round her two best girls. "Now ain't that a sight," she breathed.

Moon moths danced after the retreating stars, the Paper Moon dared another squizz, and the crowd sighed in sheer delight.

SEARCH FOR THE HEART OF THE OCEAN

Tail the Fourth:
A Chinchilla, Beasts of the Deep, and a Lost Jewel, Oh My!

THE NORTH WIND STOOD to attention as the IRATE vessel *Impolite Fortune* sailed past the headlands towards adventure.

Captain Cinrak the Dapper, capybara pirate extraordinaire, breathed it all in, her mind's eye turning the scene into words she could slip to a bard for the perfect opening of an Epic that should— would—be written if—when—Cinrak returned with her jewelled prize.

The grinning waves. The beaming sun. The figurehead meant to represent and yet not represent Rat Queen Orvillia straining to be off, reaching to embrace the open ocean. There, atop Shag Rock, chiffon streaming, Loquolchi, First Marmot Diva of the Theatre Rat-oyal, shrilling out the 'Ode to the Ocean'. Before, on the docks, Loquolchi telling Cinrak she better come home alive or so help her, she'd kill Cinrak herself.

And the *Impolite Fortune* herself, gleaming hard as the jewel she was setting out to find.

Cinrak blew her marmot lover a final farewell kiss, then saluted claw to brow for the North Wind's spectacular contribution.

"Everything ship shape and ready to be fancy free, ser," said First Mate Riddle, a patchwork rat, snapping a salute forepaw to chest.

"Open her up, Riddle m'lass."

"Yes, ser!" Riddle slipped her eyepatch to the other side and glared with an empty eye socket down the deck. "You heard the cap! Let 'er fly!"

The excited crew sang open the snapping sails which whispered taunts to the North Wind. As the breeze stiffened, Cinrak clutched her portfolio tighter. The North Wind could get frisky when excited. It would do her no good to lose star-turns of hard-won secrets to the greedy water.

One pouting snout stood out. Riddle twitched her head towards a young grey chinchilla skulking near the down ladder. Cinrak sighed, straightened her purple paisley bow tie, and pulled at the hem of her green silk waistcoat.

Time to deal with the new cabin girl.

"With me," Cinrak growled in passing.

The girl put her head down and followed. Cinrak could almost take it as an insult, but she remembered well her own first sun on an IRATE vessel.

Cabin door clicked shut. Desk drawer lock clicked, hiding the portfolio. The pirates of IRATE loved each other, but at the end of the sun they were still pirates.

Cinrak drummed forepaw claws on the immaculate desk top.

"Competition be fierce for the apprenticeship you be doin'," she said. "Ev'ry cabin girl from the *Impolite Fortune* have become respected commanders in the IRATE fleet. Ye balance looks good, m'girl, but your mind be elsewhere."

The little chinchilla folded her arms. She was of age to serve with IRATE, but her thin arms, delicate paws, and drooping whiskers needed plenty of discipline to deal with the heavy work and merciless weather.

"Yes, ser," the grey chinchilla sighed.

"Minerva, is it?" The girl looked away, clenched her jaw. Cinrak thought of how the youngling had winced when her mother had smothered her in farewell kisses. "I promised yer m'arm you'd be in fine and safe paws. An' that comes with the IRATE life-time guarantee. But you gotta work with me here, Minerva. If it be a boy or a girl or a school or a desert caravan that be callin' yer name, ye betta be tellin' me now. Us IRATE pirates not be takin' disrespect."

The restless and heavy silence grew, getting itchy around the edges.

Deepest Depths, thought Cinrak. Maybe it would be best if I dropped this little one off at the next port.

The chinchilla burst out, "It's not that I don't want to be here, ser!" Then she looked everywhere for her escaping words.

Cinrak sat back. "Go awn." She gestured towards a stool. The girl slumped down with a sigh.

"I do respect the Independent Rodent Aquatic Trade Entente, oh, I do, ser!" The chinchilla found her animation, black eyes gleaming. "I've wanted nothing more to be a pirate and serve on the *Impolite Fortune* and meet the people of the deep since I was a wee one, but I..."

Something familiar in the set of her whiskers, something deep in her dark eyes, made Cinrak decide. "I be listenin'. That's what a good captain does."

The chinchilla lifted her chin, flicked her whiskers once. "I am not who my m'arm told you I am. My name is Benj, and I am a *boy*. A cabin boy. If that means I must be displaced from serving on the *Impolite Fortune*, so be it. But please, ser. I do so want to meet the mers. And there's something about the ocean, something out there, I can...smell it. If you must, set me ashore again, just *don't send me back home*."

Cinrak blinked once. Oh. A lost boy. This was *much* easier to deal with than a homesick apprentice.

"Deepest Depths, Benj. On Orvillia's Crown, I swear yer most welcome here. The *Impolite Fortune* welcomes crew of many genders an' fluidities. Ye be need guidance of that nature, talk to Cookie. Or second mate Zupe, they like to be a boy sometimes."

A sigh like a great weight left Benj, and on the return breath, his chest swelled up. His smile finally crept in, if a little late to the party. "And you?" he said in a tiny voice.

Cinrak straightened her bow tie. "I be happy to teach you a thing or two 'bout dapperness. It in me name."

"Ser, *thank you*, ser."

"Now. Go find First Mate Riddle. She be showing ye how to make bunk. Then see what supplies Cookie needs run fer dinner."

"Yes, *ser!*" Benj's salute smacked whip smart against the breast of his leather jerkin.

"And Benj?"

"Yes, ser?"

"We be makin' a pirate of ye before this mission is over, and ye'll earn your name addendum."

"Yes, ser!"

The cabin door slammed and the room winced.

Cinrak chuckled and retrieved the secret portfolio. Maybe she'd become more ship m'arm than captain to the boy, but thems the wave breaks.

THE SHADOW TRAILING THE *Impolite Fortune* made Cinrak nervous, and it took a lot to make her nervous.

And this shadow was a *lot*: too succinct to be cloud reflection, too precise to be a fish roil. Too early for whales this far south, and too far off shore for a bank of inktons.

Cinrak didn't believe in monsters, except when she did.

Three suns past Merholm, the shadow dissipated when Cinrak gathered the crew on deck for an evening feast. Everyone came dressed in their best frills and frocks, silks and stockings. Deck feasts were a prelude to some important announcement, and the *Impolite Fortune's* turn of direction had had the crew muttering for suns. They heartily tucked into the platters of chilli or lemon doused fish, paella, cornbread, and orange grain pancakes. Cinrak decided to wait until they were well into their cups of cinnamon rum and honey whiskey before making her case.

As she practised her speech in her head, her gaze fell on Benj; he was a good, fluffy boy, faithful to mer-hair anemone tea. Cinrak often found him on deck late at night staring moonily down at the swift-still water, a cup of the sweet red beverage in his forepaw. It even sounded like he was whispering to the Paper Moon when it peeped shyly from behind clouds. He wouldn't be the first apprentice to have a sweet love affair with the delicate celestial.

Cinrak banged her cup for attention.

"As ye can see by how well the North Wind blows, our journey didna end with the entente renegotiations at Merholm. I hope ye all enjoyed yer time partakin' of the archipelago's wonders, and gettin' acquainted with our mer friends."

While the crew hollered and whistled, Benj blushed. The charming mers had fascinated him, and he'd spent hours in their library stuffing sea lore into his small big brain.

"But that be only the first phase of our mission," Cinrak continued. "I be sorry to inform ye, we be not on a mappin' and patrol of the southern coasts."

"Coast five suns back-thataway," someone yelled, and others laughed.

Cinrak took a deep breath. "I be blunt. The mission we undertake is a folly of my ego. The journey be difficult, treacherous, and one into the unknown. One which, in the end, will restore Queen Orvillia's crown to its rightful place of beauty an' style 'mongst all the great jewels in the land. She be deservin' only the best since I broke it asunder. Therefore, I go in search of... the Heart of the Ocean."

Excitement rippled through the crew. Not a strand of fur moved on Benj's body.

"I be not expectin' any o' this crew to fall in line with my wild schemes. As always, once ye assessed the rules of engagement, ye be more than welcome to dissent. There still be opportunity to make a swing towards the Gargan Peninsular, and I'll let any crew member off at Gigantia and collect them on the way back."

"That's if we come back," Riddle joked.

Cinrak let the feels have the run of the place for a moment: laughter, drinks swilling, quills and teeth and claws clicking, voices chittering.

"But ser," broke in one of the deckpaws. "The greatest jewel in the world is said to be guarded by the the fearsome kraken, as tall as the queen's castle with tentacles longer than ten vessels nose to tail!"

"Which is why, m'dear, we not be partakin' of the flesh of the inkton," Cinrak explained. "Kraken's cousins have proven intelligent and good friends of rodentkind. Friends not be eatin' friends. The mer archives tell us, yes, once beasts of Kraken's size did exist. It be not our place to tempt the Depth's wrath."

The entire crew undulated two digits in a v shape of warding. Except Benj whose black eyes widened, and he sat straight up. Cinrak hoped superstition would come to him soon. All good pirates needed it.

Cinrak continued. "After star-turns of research an' consultation with mer scholars, a bit of falling on the good side of Our Chaotic Lady, an' a touch of ego, I come to the conclusion we must go to the Edge of the World."

This knocked the air out of the crew and the North Wind. The South Wind kept its own council, and a good right it had to do so. The oceans did not give up their secrets lightly.

"The *edge* of the world, ser?" someone yelled. "Everyone knows the world is round. Just look at them horizon!"

Someone else shushed them with 'read a book of human-tales.'

Cinrak stilled the rabble by holding up a forepaw. Benj's whiskers quivered, emphasizing his stillness.

"The Edge of the World not be a myth or a human-tale. It be a riddle which points towards a great force of the natural world."

Now Benj's eyes were bulging out of his skull. Disappointment chipped out a little of Cinrak's pride. She had hoped the cabin boy would be tougher than this.

Someone tapped Cinrak on the shoulder.

No. All crew were at the table.

Some*thing* tapped Cinrak on the shoulder.

A shiny wet tentacle slid into Cinrak's vision. And kept going. And going. Undulating up onto the *Impolite Fortune's* deck.

As the quivering Paper Moon pulled a cloud across its face and the rising Moth Moon peeked over the horizon, the crew dissolved into screaming, flailing chaos.

THE KRAKEN HAD A long, globular, and moist name.

"But she says you can call her "Agnes" until you get the hang of the rest of it," Benj said, stroking a tentacle tip. The tentacle wriggled gently. A single castle window-sized eye peeped over the rail. The kraken's orange spade-shaped head went up and up and up, slicing against the blue sky.

Cinrak closed her eyes for a moment, pretending she was below decks with the rest of the crew. If one couldn't see the beast maybe it would stop existing. It hit Cinrak: Benj hadn't been mooning at the water all those nights, he'd been talking to the kraken! Cinrak strained her ears in Agnes' direction, but all she could detect was a hum like the wind strumming its favourite tune in the riggings.

"What be—" she attempted and failed the full name. "—er, Agnes wanting?"

"She's excited that someone came looking for her," he said. "She wants to help you find the Heart of the

Ocean. She's lost it too. She's lonely, and she says it's nice to have friends round these parts."

This was all a bit too much. The tiny cabin boy translating for a monster who would barely make a morsel of him. The *Impolite Fortune* tracked all this time. A lonely monster of the Depths becalming the ship with a hug. Her reputation wouldn't live it down if word spread that Cinrak the Dapper had almost wet her second-best pair of pants.

"Agnes wants to know why you're looking for the Heart?" Benj said, quiet, like he was apologizing. Agnes blinked affirmation, her eyelid nicking a few splinters off the railing.

Cinrak straightened her vest and bow tie. Despite the big fright, she was proud of Benj. She didn't know well how ocean or star magic worked, but perhaps there was a bit of the chinchilla in the kraken, or the other way around. Honesty, a pirate's mainstay, was the best solution.

"As I be responsible for breakin' apart Queen Orvillia's crown to set free the Star of a Thousand Star-Turns, I bear responsibility for replacin' the crown jewel with something equally, if not more, magnificent. The fabled Heart of the Ocean be the perfect solution. A prize worthy of Cinrak the Dapper and the Queen's legend. But if Agnes is the Heart's guardian, I be more'n willing to negotiate custody of the jewel."

A few more of the crew had crept above deck, rodent faces vacillating between dread and wonder.

Large tentacles wiggled, setting the startled ocean a-slosh. Benj chewed his whiskers, absent-mindedly stroking the tentacle. "Agnes says there may be the possibility of a deal."

Cinrak beamed.

"There's a slight problem. The riddle of the Edge of the World. It's not much of a riddle at all."

The crew held their breath.

"It is, in fact, a gigantic whirlpool."

The crew groaned.

Fear swirled in Cinrak's broad chest, but she reminded herself a good captain only showed enough fear to display how they'd overcome it.

"As I suspected." Cinrak took a deep breath. "Aye, if Agnes be so kind as to cease cuddlin' the ship, we may get underway to assess the problem."

The tentacles shivered in apology and released the ship. The riggings sighed, the Paper Moon peeked out from behind a cloud, and the North Wind whistled softly in relief.

"Agnes says you will have never seen a drain such as this one. Those of her ilk who weren't killed by it have simply...left. She is the last." Both kraken and chinchilla gestured towards the excitable stars popping into existence. "There is an additional problem. The drain is encapsulated by the Bruise."

The crew and ship groaned louder.

"Ahh, the riddle wrapped in an enigma! So that be what that great storm hides. Aye, Captain Cinrak the Dapper has never been one to swim away from a challenge. Nor is she one to leave a friend in distress. Whether they be friend on the ocean or in the ocean, we can always come to an amicable agreement."

Life fell into a strange routine as the great kraken joined the retinue. Thrill-fear lifted Cinrak's fur every time she caught a glimpse of the fabled beast leading them on. Agnes knew nothing of borders — the ocean was Everything and Everywhere for her. She turned them due south towards where even the heartiest of maties feared to sail.

Though the North Wind quivered at the peril it pushed them towards, the beneficial weather took them beyond Here Be Dragons. Cinrak would not allow her crew to be lulled into a false sense of complacency. They did storm drills every sun.

Eventually, Agnes won over the timid crewmembers. By sun, she would intimidate balls of fish towards the ship, so they never went hungry. At night, she provided shadow puppetry with the assistance of the exuberant Moth Moon. Benj watched on, proud as a parent, rapping out a beat on a drum. He didn't seem in thrall to the kraken. In fact, beneath the salt-steel that was becoming his pirate way, there remained a gentleness Cinrak couldn't help but admire.

Try as she might with all the languages of the ocean and sky, Cinrak couldn't taste the magic of this ocean creature. When Benj was otherwise occupied, Agnes demonstrated her easy power to Cinrak, chasing sea things with big teeth. Once, Cinrak watched fascinated and horrified as Agnes casually cronched a shark, tearing them apart with terrifying efficiency and feeding the struggling beast into the concentric carnassial circles.

THE BRUISE.

Cinrak smelled the broken, heavy air through darkness even before the oily storm wall slid its silky claws over the horizon. The rest of the crew woke to the odious clouds to go with their hardtack and tea.

Even Agnes hesitated, swimming agitated circles around the ship. The crew tried to ignore it; she had become something of a mascot and even the timidest crewmember had respect for her oceanly talents.

Cinrak ordered the anchor dropped, and started her calculations all over again. The storm was bigger than rumour had suggested. The roar of the wind and drain was audible even at a safe distance and above the determined heave-ho songs of the crew.

"What says Agnes?"

Cinrak found Benj in his usual spot by the figurehead. He'd knotted a green scarf to represent his growing rope skills and respect for his captain's Dapperly Arts. Along with his new muscles and groomed fur, she couldn't help but be proud of her protégé.

Benj's smile gave no assurance. "Brave is scribed in her blood, ser, but I can tell she is a little...concerned. She says the whirlpool has grown since she was here last."

Cinrak repressed a sigh. She had hoped out of all involved, Agnes would have some idea of how to penetrate the boiling purple and blue clouds stabbed with eager lightning. It was not like Cinrak the Dapper to back out of a challenge, but she had the whole crew to think about. Best take a hit to her reputation than a hit to the *Impolite Fortune*.

A cough.

"Sorry to barge in, ser, but you'll be wanting to see this," Riddle said, unpatched eye hot with hope.

The crew parted to let the captain and cabin boy through. The sun beamed a spotlight on a mer sitting precariously on the starboard railing combing out his waist length auburn beard and hair.

"Captain Cinrak!" The mer air-kissed Cinrak's cheeks. "So lovely to see you!"

"Cut the starfish poop," Cinrak grinned. "Yer a long way from home."

"Our scouts informed us you'd made it this far *and* that you had a friend in tow." Colombia winked at Agnes who blinked back, her eyelid sending a curious dolphin scurrying.

"You knew a kraken still swims." Cinrak folded her arms.

Colombia took no offence. "Of course. We're all friends in the waters. Honestly, we didn't think dear—" Colombia pronounced Agnes' full name with ease. "—was associated with any of this." He gestured towards the boiling storm. Agnes waved back.

"So why she be attachin' herself to the *Impolite Fortune's* fortune?" Cinrak asked. "What be so different about our attempt to sail over the Edge of the

World and retrieve the Heart of the Ocean compared to all other ships that failed?"

Colombia leaned forward and looked up through his long lowered lashes. "Magic."

Cinrak threw up her forepaws. "Deepest Depths!"

"It's true." Colombia combed out a hair knot. "She can taste it on the ship."

In her head, Cinrak catalogued the small charms she kept in her cabin and the abilities of her crew. Some of them, like her, had small skills in weather work, but nothing that could soothe such a storm and certainly nothing on a wizard's level. That meant...

"Benj?"

"Me?" The cabin boy trembled.

"So it's you who can talk to her." Colombia's sharp grin turned on Benj. "Congratulations. One in a hundred star-turns."

"M...Me?"

Colombia placed a meaty, hairy webbed hand on Benj's shoulder. "You're made of stars, m'boy. Tell me what you can taste on the air."

The crew stepped back as Benj closed his eyes and took a deep breath.

"Emptiness," Benj intoned, his voice taking on a deeper timbre. With the health benefits of Night Rose tea, Cinrak knew he'd come through puberty fine. "A black hole that goes deep into the...no, not the ocean or the earth. Into a void, a nothing. There's water there, but it's not water." His furry forehead screwed up at the contradiction. "I can feel...far away, a heart beating."

Cinrak's fists and jaw ached. The jewel, pulsing under some beautiful light! So close! But so far!

"Good, good," Colombia soothed, iridescent fin tips twitching with delight. "What else? Spread your senses wider. Soar up, like the star you are."

"The water we can see, is...not as smooth as we're lead to believe. It...runs rapidly across ragged rocks. Huh." Benj opened his eyes. "So that's what those old maps in the library meant."

"Explain," Riddle asked.

Thinking of her secret maps, Cinrak nodded as Benj spoke.

"Thousands of star-turns ago, there used to be a series of merholm scattered far out into ocean," Colombia explained, serious as a swordfish. "But the ocean never sleeps. Volcanos, glaciers, heat, cold. Those islands are now underwater. What we know as coastline has been changing and will keep changing, so slow you can't see it. But sometimes, like the Edge and Bruise here, very fast."

"For ev'ry magical action, there be a natural reaction," Cinrak said.

"Correct," Colombia said. "Just like you can't take a star from the sky and put it into the queen's crown without the stars being upset."

Cinrak grimaced.

"Oh, my dear heart!" Benj gasped, leaning far out over the railing. "Why didn't you tell me?"

Agnes dipped low in the water, the tip of her remorseful eye peeking out.

"Tell ye what?" Cinrak asked, heart already aching.

"Magic made this mess! Agnes worked with her beloved, Xolotli, to protect the Heart," Benj said. "But even the best and longest of loves can go through rocky times, and they had a, uh, disagreement about how best to protect the great Heart from pirates. In a fit of anger, Xolotli banished Agnes from their ocean home. Xolotli's agitation was so great the Edge formed above them, preventing Agnes from returning once her temper had cooled."

The crew either snuffled or attempted to look staunch. It was a love story for the ages.

Colombia chimed in. "None of the other kraken-kind could help Agnes because the Edge was too strong. They all eventually departed the ocean for the stars, perhaps attempting to find a solution."

"She's been swimming the oceans for hundreds of star-turns, alone?" Riddle wailed into her kerchief. "That's terrible! Cap'n, we have to *do* something!"

Cinrak chewed her whiskers. "Even with me best calculations one ship couldna possibly hope to defeat the storm, let alone survive the drop into the drain."

"The rocks!" Benj gasped, his eyes widening. He turned to Colombia. "You said the old merholm were submerged, but some of them would have had hills and mountains that would be near the surface now, yes?"

"We've swum around a few and collected artifacts and samples," Colombia confirmed. "But the closer to the drain, the more treacherous it becomes. Even a group of strong mer linked together can't battle such a current."

Benj whirled to his captain. "You still have your famous merhair rope that helped you win the race of the stars, Cap'n?"

"O' course." She brought it out as her best boast on rare occasions. "But it be only a ten span at best."

"But it is a link to the stars."

Colombia nodded. "We come from the same material as kraken and stars."

"Air, ocean, made of the same stuff, just different states." Benj's eyes shone like the stars. "With Agnes' strength, the merhair rope, the crew's skill, and a series of underwater tethers, we might be able to make our way into the drain. *Together.*"

"I'm going to sing up a few extra nearby scouts," Colombia said as he plopped down into the water. Agnes patted him as gently as she could on the head. "A little extra muscle wouldn't go amiss. If that is all right by you, Cap'n."

All eyes turned to Cinrak. She shrugged and grinned. "Do'na look at me. Seems Benj and Agnes have this well in paw."

Benj bounced in place and clapped his forepaws. "Let's get Agnes back together with her beloved!"

The crew cheered. Agnes waved a half-dozen tentacles.

Cinrak rubbed her forepaws in anticipation. The most precious jewel in the world was so close, she could almost taste its glittering candy facets and the eternal gratitude of her queen.

CINRAK DIDN'T KNOW WHERE the wind's scream ended and the crew's cries and the ship's tortured creaks began.

The first tetherings and tentative excursion into the outer rim of the storm had gone well. Both anchors were linked to merhair, which was linked to Agnes, who held fast to underwater rocky pillars and swung them further inwards. But now the crew and mer scouts were tiring. There wasn't any rain, but the crashing waves kept everyone soaked.

Strapped to the figurehead, Benj yelled instructions as Agnes inched along the submerged rocks. Having an enormous eye upon the precariously close ocean floor made things a little easier, though every channel was a close call.

A jerk, a groan of anchors, and a sudden flash-clamber of iridescent scales as the merfolk tumbled on board.

"What gives!" yelled Cinrak through her boomer from her place in the crow's nest.

"Current is too much!" Colombia yelled back. "It's all Agnes from here on in!"

"She be all right?" Cinrak called to Benj.

Benj lifted his own boomer. "She's hating it! And loving it! This is the furthest she's ever made it into the drain!"

"Tell her she can stop at any point. Her safety comes first!"

Benj saluted understanding.

The *Impolite Fortune* shuddered forward through another narrow channel.

A hundred nights fell all at once over the ship, and thunder pressed its invisible paws against Cinrak's ears. But this thunder kept going and going and *going*. The dark sound laughing them into the storm's maw was no beast; here was the gigantic drain, an intertwining of magic and nature writ large.

The world seemed to simply *end*. The spinning water fell into a darkness so complete the night sky would die from envy. It swallowed everything: sucking the soul out of what remained of light, flinging the shrieks of the crew down and stomping on them, tearing breath from chest leaving only iron-salt fear on the back of the throat.

This was it. The Edge of the World, leading to the Void. A nothing. A thoroughfare to death.

But there. A flicker. A tiny sliver of silver promise. A throb. Another. A flutter of light to hold hope close.

Way down below. The Heart of the Ocean. Beating.

The crew lashed the mers to themselves and tied all to the inner cargo rings. Cinrak had never known rodents and mer to work in such harmony before. It was a beautiful sight amongst chaos.

"That's it," Benj boomed. "That's as far as Agnes can go! It's all down from here!"

"Deepest Depths, deliver us safely to your soft shores," Cinrak invoked through gritted teeth.

The timbers of the *Impolite Fortune* creaked such a protest, tears sprang to Cinrak's eyes. Was this it for her dearest ship? Was the best beavercraft in the business falling apart?

And what of poor Agnes? Was she tearing apart down there too?

Aaaaaghhhrooooohhhhhhhh.

A great groan rose, diamond hard pressure against Cinrak's senses.

The Depths...were answering her plea?

Aaaaarrrrrrooooooooohnnnnggggh.

No, there was Agnes, her great eye gleaming as bright as a constellation of starfish on summer solstice.

"Strap yourself down!" Benj shouted. "She's gonna let go the tether!"

Aaoooooogggggahhhh.

"What?!"

"We're going in!"

Cinrak's paws burned as she slid down the guide rope. She whisked the cabin boy the last few meters and tied them both to the scurry of crew.

Ooooooooooaaaaarrrhh.

"What is that?!" Cinrak yelled.

"The call of the ocean!" Colombia cried, ecstatic.

"Deepest Depths, that's something *living!*"

"The ocean lives!"

"It's Agnes' beloved!" Benj yelled.

"They'd be too far down..."

"Here we go!"

The world tilted. The boat and crew screamed in unison.

Falling forever, into a silence so profound it could write its own Epic.

Tiny glimmers of light rose from the depths of the Void, like sunrise on the edge of whiskers.

A coruscation of green-purple-blue from ceph-alopod skin, tentacles curving over every possible edge of the ship. Agnes cuddled the *Impolite Fortune* as, impossibly, the kraken and ship floated in mid-air.

Cinrak blinked at the dancing sparkles. They reminded her of racing stars running backwards. The air tasted of petrichor and an indefinable sweet tang, like oranges, sword blades, and kisses all mushed into one.

"Whu...?" She blundered.

Some of the crew blubbered. A few silently wept. Most gazed in awe.

Ooooooohhhhhaaarrrhhhoooo crooned the moan. It came from all around now.

The sparkles moved upwards faster and it took Cinrak a moment to realize the stars weren't moving, the *ship* was. Going down down down. What sort of cushion would Agnes make for the biggest frigate of the IRATE fleet? Probably a very squishy one. They'd never get the smell of squid out of the drapes.

She was dead, Cinrak decided. Definitely dead. And Loquolchi would have her guts for garters.

A gentle bump put paid to Cinrak's cleaning nightmare. The *Impolite Fortune* protested audibly as Agnes withdrew her embrace, but the kraken took not one splinter with her. The ship settled into its new medium with a sigh of contentment.

When Cinrak dared a look, the light from the uncountable stars showed a medium rippling like water, giving way like cool molten glass under her touch, but not wet. The ocean-that-was-not-ocean Benj had burbled about.

"Deepest Depths," Cinrak breathed.

"Indeed," Colombia sighed, hands clasped in front of his hairy breast, smile as big as a sunfish. "That *is* where we are."

Oooooooohhhhhhaahhhhh affirmed the occupant of the endless sky-under-ocean.

A beast even more enormous than Agnes swum above, around, below in the not-water. Rainbows shimmered across see-through skin, which revealed pulsating, squirming organs in gorgeous jewel tones. Spine and skull curved like the finest of marble carvings, and it was strange to see the beauty in their movement as whalebone was usually only viewed in the repose of death.

"It's a glass whale," Benj sighed.

"We thought they were all extinct." Tears shimmered in Colombia's beard. "Gone to the skies with their kraken-siblings."

Agnes whirled around the undulating glass whale, tentacles describing things too large and delicate for rodents and mers to understand.

Cinrak too took a moment to enjoy being alive. Her ship had survived, though some of the sails and her green silk vest were in tatters. At the beautiful sight of lovers reunited, the crew danced and wept, the mers slapped their tails and sang. Benj watched on with a beatific smile bending his whiskers, paws clenching and unclenching in time to the tentacular spectacular.

Cinrak waited. She had spent a long time searching for the Heart of the Ocean, but Agnes had spent much longer away from her beloved. A few more moments before the jewel was in her paws wouldn't matter.

With a relenting, soft *arrrooooggghhh*, the glass whale allowed Agnes to wrap her arms around them. The embrace was so delicate and loving for such huge beasts, stray tears on her furry cheeks caught Cinrak by surprise.

Benj grinned. "Agnes says their name is still Xolotli."

Cinrak paused in winding a rope. "Still?"

Colombia sucked his whiskers. Something like comprehension snuck thief-like across his face. "I think...it would change if something was taken away from here."

"The Heart," Cinrak nodded. "That makes sense. They be the guardian of the jewel."

An upward lilting *arroogh*. An affirmation. Did the whale understand rodent tongue?

"Get to it, ye lot," Cinrak coughed. "We needin' to be ship shape so we be figurin' how to get back up top."

The crew were sluggish to turn away from the sight of the wondrous reunion between the beasts, but to their credit, they held fast to their IRATE values: ship first.

"Alright. I guess there bein' a cave or a chest or a pedestal round here," Cinrak murmured to Benj and Riddle.

"It's in a chest..." The cabin boy started to say, and that was all Cinrak needed. She sent Riddle scampering to launch the captain's sculler.

"But, ser," Benj tried again, tugging on her arm.

Cinrak frowned him into silence. "We've upheld our end of the bargain, now it be Agnes' turn."

"No! You can't!" Benj blurted, front teeth showing. He was perilously close to insubordination.

"We problee do'na be havin' much time, Benj. Now the anger an' magic of them hundreds o' star-turns be dissipatin', that drain'll collapse in on itself. We do'na wanna be here when that happens."

But Benj planted his rear paws and folded his arms, whiskers aquiver. "No!"

Cinrak's nostrils flared. "Benj," she growled, straightening to her full capybara height.

Benj planted his small self between the captain and the unfurled rope ladder. "You can't have the Heart!"

Colombia and the mer scouts gathered at the rail, looking between the unfolding scenes in the not-water and on board. The rest of the crew put their heads down and made busy. They all knew that look on their captain's face.

"This ain't a negotiation," Cinrak growled. "Agnes promised."

"To *lead* you to the Heart, not let you cut it out of the ocean!" Benj was on the verge of tears, but to his credit he stood his ground. Cinrak would keep that in mind when she decided his punishment.

Chest puffed, Cinrak stepped face to face with the cabin boy. "I ain't arguing with ye. Under IRATE law, a deal is a deal. You gotta be learnin' to toughen up that heart a' yours, boy."

A gasp, like a spring breeze across a prickleberry bush. The mers. *Propriety be damned*, she thought. Cinrak the Dapper's reputation came as salty as the ocean.

Forceful in her anger, Cinrak swung about to face the judgment of her mer friends and smacked snout to wet leathery appendage.

Agnes reared up over the ship, eye apologetic but tentacles an impenetrable wall. Whichever way Cinrak tried to dodge, the tentacle in her face followed.

Benj placed himself between the tentacle and his captain. "Agnes says you can't have the Heart of the Ocean."

"But she promised!"

Benj pointed at the now relaxed glass whale blowing curious spouts. Such a sight, water in, water out. "*There* is your chest with your prize. It is an *actual* chest. An *actual* heart!"

"Oh." The entirety of the revelation replaced Cinrak's breath with silence.

And what a beautiful heart it was. An enormous, scintillating ruby shot through with veins of sapphire and pink diamond. It pumped prodigiously, pushing plasma through the plump pellucid physique.

"Well." Cinrak coughed around a plethora of emotions. "We ca'na be puttin' that in the queen's crown now, can we?"

XOLOTLI HAD OCEAN MAGIC to spare. From what Cinrak could ascertain from Benj's loving burbles, the whirlpool had gotten away from her, the power of the Void self-sustaining. Now that she had her love and control back, she deftly broke the bonds on the Edge of the World and let the drain disperse. The *Impolite Fortune* rode the ocean wall up and up, supported again by the soft weight of Agnes' tentacles.

The strange star-like lights sunk back into the depths, embraced by the Void like an impenetrable night flipped on its head. Cinrak's heart wanted to flow with them. It made her feel so small and yet so large at the same time. The stars still had lessons to teach her.

Upon reaching the surface, the mers began whistling in excitement. The dissipation of the water walls had revealed the submerged archipelago. The mer quickly rescued gaping fish and set to exploring the seaweed-draped ruins.

While the crew and mers fussed over the persistence of their respective homes, Benj sat atop the highest point on the main island, silent and strong as a masthead. Agnes and Xolotli swum excited circles around each other and the islands. With the Bruise gone and the ocean calm, the tableau glittered iridescent beneath the excited Moth and Paper Moons and stars.

Cinrak approached her cabin boy carefully, forepaws crossed across her broad chest. "I, yuh, have come teh apologize."

The wee chinchilla's eyes widened at the unexpected opening. "Why? You're the Captain. You make calls as you see fit."

"But I didna listen to ye. I bin so focused on my reward, agin. I wouldna ever be hurtin' a creature to take what I be needin' or wantin'. 'Specially one so beautiful as Xolotli."

A wistful sigh escaped between Benj's whiskers. "They are that." Belatedly, he stood and snapped a salute, fur making a damp little squish beneath his fist. "But in the end, you failed to get what you promised."

"Neh." Cinrak shrugged. "Ye learn to make the best o' a situation. I found the Edge of the Earth, tamed the great whirlpool, and reunited lovers. That in itself will be makin' a great Epic I can sell to the bards for star-turns to come. An' look. The mers have found a part of their lost home. They be happy too."

"But what about the queen's crown? Won't she be mad?"

"She'll get over it. 'Sides, sometimes I be thinkin' a jewel ain't what make a leader great. Orvillia is a good ratty, but she be needin' to find her own heart, an' not be takin' it from the ocean. Or the land."

Benj stared at his captain, open-mouthed. Cinrak chuckled and slapped him on the back. "Eh, let me be tellin' you 'bout ogre socialism sometime, young kit."

Agnes forestalled any further brusque sentimentality by rising high in the water, tentacles flailing as the mers whistled and laughed.

"What be botherin' her now?" Cinrak asked.

"Well, er, she has a gift for you, ser."

"Does she now."

Agnes swam as close as she dared and Cinrak clambered down the slippery rocks to greet her. "This gift better not be a hug," she grumbled.

Agnes unfurled a leathery tentacle, the tip ending perfectly before Cinrak's blunt snout. Balanced on the tip was a jewel the size of Cinrak's fist, striated with perfect sweet rosiness, a flash of diamond star, and a blue as dark as the deepest ocean. It smelled like the crackle-taste of stars.

"She says...oh." Benj gasped sweetly. "It's a piece of whalefall from the deepest trench. It's been down there for so long, the pressure of the water and remnants of its sky cousins have rendered it into something new."

"Like pieces of the earth deep in the earth," Colombia said, coming closer to inspect the proffered gift.

"Whale goop and star poop," Benj giggled.

"A piece of dead whale turned jewel," Cinrak breathed, touching a claw tip to the stone. Sure enough, it tingled like the star had tingled beneath her thighs when she rode it. "How marvelous. I never be thinkin' o' such a thing. Are ye sure?"

Agnes blinked and shook the tentacle a little: *here, take it.*

Cinrak took the stone and rolled it gently between her forepaws. It gave off a warmth unexplained by the eons spent below in the freezing dark. "What part of the whale it bein'?"

"Heart," Benj said.

An enormous whale heart compacted down to this? Cinrak saluted and bowed to Agnes who waved her tentacles back. "Yer kindness will never be for-gotten—" She clicked and slurped her way through the full name.

She slipped the stone into the Alice pocket of her vest for safekeeping. So, she got her heart after all. Did she deserve it? What had she just said about jewels and crowns and queens? She needed to think on this one.

The North Wind, having searched frantically all around the Bruise since the ship disappeared, finally found them and blew a warm sigh of relief. Xolotli blew rainbows, the ocean kissed the stones, and the *Impolite Fortune* groaned through its litany of aches.

"All aboard!" Cinrak called.

When she reached the railing, she looked down to find Benj gathered with the mers who were staying to investigate the uncovered islands.

"Hey!" she called. "It be time to go!"

From the rise in his now tatty vest and scarf, Cinrak could see Benj was gathering his courage.

"I think—" His voice cracked downwards. "I'm staying here. Agnes needs me."

Perhaps, Cinrak thought, it was the other way round.

Benj continued, "The mers need me too." Colombia slapped him on the shoulder with his long fin and nodded. "What I learned back in Merholm, what I've learned from Agnes and Xolotli and my m...magic. My place, for now, is here."

There was no use in giving a speech about IRATE duty, but Cinrak gave it anyway, out of duty. Riddle collected Benj's kit from below deck and threw it down.

"Not sure how you gonna keep it all dry though!" she laughed.

"I'll learn quick," Benj grinned, saluting the first mate.

Something pinched hard in Cinrak's chest. Her own jewel-like heart, dusting off memories of discovering bow ties and girls and ocean delights? Or a little throb of the whale heart hidden in her vest?

"Take care, ye salty wee scrapper," Cinrak called as they cast off. "We be back soon, ye can count on that. Not fair ye get to have all the fun! Oh, an' Benj? I got ye pirate name! A-Benj the Ocean Star!"

He laughed at the pun. "It's perfect! Thank you!"

"Yer welcome."

"Give my best to Orvillia and Loquolchi!" Benj roar-squeaked, tears in his eyes.

"That's *Queen* Orvillia to you, young mer-fur," Colombia chuckled.

The shimmer of mer and whale song followed the *Impolite Fortune* for as long as the stars stitched the sky together. As dawn peaked over the horizon and the sun sparkled a yawn, sending the Moth and Paper Moon off to their beds, the glass whale blew one final rainbow salute and Agnes made intricate signs with her tentacles Cinrak thought she could almost read.

One more salute to kraken and whale and Cinrak wiped her salty-sweet cheeks dry and turned her snout towards where her two other loves made home.

THE HIRSUTE PURSUIT

Tail the Fifth:
To the Mountain,
to See How Hairy It Is

HORNS HARPED ACROSS THE Ratholme harbour. Cider grew warm and cushions cold at The Bloody Mary Tavern. Ships swarmed with scurrying sailors. Dolphins danced in the dappled sunlit waves, squeeing out their message.

The Beard of Covetona Island had returned.

Cinrak the Dapper, capybara captain of the pirate vessel the *Impolite Fortune*, issued a multitude of orders. She waved her arms with an excitement that mirrored the waving tentacles of Agnes the kraken when she had blasted into the harbour. A tense moment between Cinrak and the city guard rushing with their harpoons ensued as she translated via her cabin kit Benj, Agnes' mind-kin, that the enormous beast brought a message of goodwill. The dolphins had seen the hair of the Covetona volcano, gossiped to Agnes, and together they came to tell Rodentdom of the once in a lifetime harvest.

107

A harvest Cinrak was determined to be first to partake of and get the greatest take. Not for herself, but for Benj, all like him who needed to reveal their true gender, and to make sure of an equitable distribution of the resource. No hoarding by apothecaries for star-turns and price gouging on her watch.

Cinrak's barrel chest puffed out with pride as she watched Benj rush around telling anyone who would listen "I'm going to get my beard!" The crew were cheered by his infectious excitement and increased their efforts to get under the eye of the South Wind first.

Mystery shrouded Covetona. Many said the Great Capybara Mother had rested paws there during her journeys through Ratdom. Cinrak believed that as much as she believed the Great Mother ever existed. It would be quite something to be part of the Epic told about this generation's Beard Expedition and help the theologians with their questions.

The three-tone whistle of "Honoured Guest Ahoy" startled Cinrak. An elderly rat with a silver scar through one eye and a walking cane and a middle-aged capybara waited to be welcomed aboard.

Cinrak stepped down to the docks and gripped the wrist of her old mentor, Mereg the Sharp, pirate-style. "Good to be with ya, friend!"

"Greets, friend." Mereg passed over a packet of thick pages. "I found the maps ye asked for. An' another friend for ye."

Cinrak held back her grimace. It had been a good ten star-turns since she had personally delivered a tithe to her old home, but there was no mistaking that snout. "Helet."

"Hello, Cinrak. It's been a while. I understand you require my assistance." Her old guardian from the orphanage was both younger and older than she remembered, grey sprinkling her neck and ears, but back just as stick-straight as ever.

"Ah, Ratdom's finest expert on the Great Mother wantin' a piece of Covetona."

Helet beamed a long-tooth smile. "Of course I do, dear. I can tell you all about the island and those wicked wild fairies where Mereg cannot."

Mereg gripped the head of their cane with both paws, choosing to cut Helet with the daggers of their eyes than with any of the daggers secreted on their person. It wasn't their fault they couldn't sail anymore.

"Ye been there before."

"You assume correctly. One of those times Mereg was...proficient enough to escort me on my studies, we visited Covetona at harvest time. Unfortunately, the local population of fairies wouldn't allow me all the way to the top of the mountain to investigate the supposed site of the Mother's shrine."

Cinrak rubbed the bridge of her nose. It made sense to have a theological specialist along to make an official report. But Helet had a habit of sticking her snout into places she didn't belong. It would be a juggle to keep her out of pirate, and Benj's, business.

"A'ight, welcome aboard."

Helet bustled up the gangway.

A voice cut through the clatter of loading.

"Greets! My name is Benj. Pleased ta have ya aboard! You going to visit the beard too? Can you imagine it? A mountain growing a beard! I wonder how soft it is. Do you know? I'm going to get my beard!"

Helet stared at Benj's outstretched paw. She delicately pinched claw to tippy claw and jiggled it in something that was an ugly reminder of a greeting. "Oh. I recognize you now. You're Chauncy's girl. I'd heard you'd run away to sea. I didn't realize it was with my Cinrak."

Benj's entire pelt shivered. He hadn't been misgendered since he'd joined the *Impolite Fortune*.

"Ah, matron. Ye be mistakin'." Cinrak hustled up to the altercation, loading her voice with sugar. "Lad, this be me former matron, Helet. Helet, this be my cabin lad, Benj. Actually, excusin' me. Still getting used to callin' him me Fourth Mate!"

Benj's teary eyes went quite wide at the sudden promotion.

Helet looked between capybara and chinchilla and grunted. She fished around for something else to say. "And how does a chinchilla stop from *dying* when around all this water?"

"Oh, then you must meet Agnes!" Just mentioning his large orange friend brought the light back to his round face. "She's taught me a few of her tricks. There's always puff powder. And I'm not the only chinchilla that's ever been a pirate, so all vessels have dust tubs. If you'd spent any time even near a pirate vessel that would be obvious!"

Helet's snout scrunched a little as she tried to decide if she'd been insulted. "Agnes? Who is this?"

The perfect answer was a warning honk from a barge across the harbour.

"Oi! Agnes!" Cinrak called. "I ken the channels be nice 'n smooth for yer arms, but the ferries come first. Back it up."

The harbour water rippled like a rapid backwards tide. The barge honked its thanks and powered on.

The kraken's great spade-shaped head rose up at the harbour entrance and her single enormous eye blinked a sweet apology, creating a small wash that slapped the ship's sides.

"She only wants to be close to me," Benj explained for the hundredth time.

"I ken, lad. But the harbour just ain't big enough for her."

Helet was shrieking like the world was ending. The crew stared at her, confused. Mereg hid their good eye in a paw, shoulders shaking with laughter.

"It's just Agnes," Benj grumbled, slouching away to his duties. "She wouldn't hurt a starfish."

Cinrak whistled up her first mate. Helet winced at the noise, decided she was done yelling, then winced again at the site of the spiky haired rat with an eye-patch. "Riddle here will show ye to yer accommodations."

"Thank you, *dear*. I hope you have a cabin suitable. It's been so long since I've been on board such a, uh—" Helet cast an eye across the gleaming brass and wood. "*vessel*."

Riddle vibrated at the implication against her cleaning skills. "Cap'n?"

"Apologizin', friend," Cinrak said out the corner of her mouth as Helet swiped a claw along a rail and checked it for dust. "Be givin' her yer cabin. Ye can bunk in with me."

"Aye, Cap'n."

Riddle switched her patch to her good eye and gave her captain a consolatory shoulder pat for all she was about to endure. She'd heard the stories about her captain's guardian. Helet had never got over Cinrak's rejection of becoming her orphanage protégé, didn't understand her chosen family of pirates, and had never accepted Cinrak's love of marmot diva Loquolchi and the rodent queen Orvillia, the former because she was 'one of those artist types who spread herself around liberally', the latter because Cinrak would never use her pirate clout to give Helet an introduction at court.

Riddle led Helet away just as efficiently as if her good eye was uncovered. Cinrak always admired that skill in her first mate.

Cinrak clumped back down to the dock so Mereg could talk without getting green around the gills. "Talk fast, or North Wind help me, I be stickin' puffer fish in yer breakfast."

"Ye said ye needed the best to beat everyone to the beard, so I brought ye the best." Mereg tapped their walking cane. They'd fashioned it to hide a wicked thin rapier within. "She ken how them wild fairies be."

The captain and her mentor walked the length of the ship, checking the last of the supplies being hauled aboard by winch and pulley.

"But I be bettin' ye know more." Cinrak pulled at the hem of her vest in the union green and purple colours, then stopped. She'd have to pay particular attention to her frustrated tells around Helet. She would pick on *anything*.

"Here." Mereg palmed her another packet. "I wrote up all me notes. Be rememberin' that wild to them don't mean what it means to rodentkind. In old fairy dialect it mean 'O' the people'. Their ways may be different and often impenetrable to us, but it's kept 'em an' their land safe for a long time."

"Aye, aye, ser." Cinrak slapped an exaggerated paw to breastbone salute. "What ye reckon the Beard o' Covetona an' the Great Capybara Mother have in common?"

Mereg tapped their cane against a dock piling. Something twinkled deep in their eyes.

"A'ight. Don't tell me then."

"The fairies don't let anyone up to the top o' the volcano fer a reason. Respect that. For the time bein', work on what we discussed. Changin' the supply chain o' rare stuffs."

"'My table be yer table, an' there be enough places for all."

The silver scar bisecting Mereg's eye twitched. "Ye know yer Mountain Sermon. Thought ye stopped with the Great Mother as a kit."

"Chapter 2, line 3, to be precise. Still carry me a primer."

"Red cover?"

"Nay, green cover."

"A first edition? Don't be tellin' Helet ye have the liberal interpretation. Ye'll never hear the end o' it."

"Don't I know that." Cinrak whistled up a crew member to check the veracity of one of the bow lines to avoid her mentor's gaze. She would miss having Mereg at her side for an adventure of this importance, but Mereg was making the best of their balance infirmity as a full time ambassador of the International Rodent Aquatic Trade Entente and troublemaker to the queen's court. You could take the pirate off the ocean, but you could never take away their salt.

With a rush of excited air, Benj was at his captain's side again. "The Royal Inspector is ready to sign off, Cap'n. No weather magicians secreted aboard here. 'Cept yerself."

Mereg grunted a laugh. At least they could see the dry humour in this IRATE rule. They grasped Benj's shoulder before he could vibrate out of existence.

"That matron might be makin' trouble for ye, young 'un," they said, warm tone sending a tingle of memory through Cinrak. "But remember ye got yer family. Trust yer crew."

Benj beamed, enjoying the praise from his grand-mentor. He switched that glowing beam to his captain. "Is what you said true? I'm really promoted?"

"Ye deserve it, lad. Ye worked hard."

"Does this mean I'm giving up my attendance duties?" Suddenly, Benj looked far too young for the star-turns he'd spent at her side.

Cinrak clasped his other shoulder, forging him as the bridge between her and her mentor. "Not if ye don't want to, lad. Will take me a while to find a new cabin kit. Ye'll be hard to replace."

"Understood, Cap'n. And I can do double duty!" He saluted, then he was off again.

"He be a wonderful wee squiddy. Gonna have a time a'tween him an' Helet! Have fun." Mereg's cane tapped the cobbles as they limped away.

Cinrak straightened her bow tie as she struggled to straighten her attitude. Deepest Depths, what was she going to do with that contumacious capybara?

HAIR. GOLDEN COPPER AUBURN glimmering in the early morning sunshine, a river streaming to the tide's edge from the face of Covetona along an ancient cut in the jungle.

And the face was indeed a face.

Volcano vents near the island's peak formed a pattern of eyes winking with lava, nose snorting

steam, and a mouth from which the Beard orig-
inated. The whole crew exclaimed in amazement and
delight at the natural wonder, while Benj zoomed
around the deck.

Despite the tropical warmth, Cinrak shivered.
The South Wind's ice had melted from her fur, but
exhaustion made stones of her bones. The notoriously
cantankerous South Wind had to be fussed into turning
its attention to the *Impolite Fortune* with promises of a
positive depiction in the Epic that would be written
about the adventure.

It wouldn't be a southerly without icy storms,
but the South Wind had been impressed by Cinrak's
gumption and tenacity, giving them a good head start.
The trailing fleet of union and non-IRATE ships were
left to catch the scraps of wind off the sheer mountains
that rose along the northern coast which pointed
toward the Unknown Ocean, knuckles breaking up
into the fiery islands of which Covetona was one.

An Ahoy.

"Cap'n!" Riddle pointed to the beach. "A friend
appears!"

Benj rushed to the railing, squinting at the blue
shape waiting patiently at the edge of the sand. "A
wild fairy! Take me with you, captain, let me ask them
straight!"

"Nay, lad. I have ta go alone. Them's the rules."
Cinrak gave him the smile that worked on all the
crew.

"Hmph, pirate rules. They don't usually hold much water." Helet squinted across the morning-bright water.

Cinrak's face ached as she held her smile in place. She and her old guardian had bickered all the way. Helet continued to speak to her as if she was still her orphan charge. To the rest of the crew, the snipes and jibes may have been meaningless, what any family engaged in. But Helet only gave lip service to the concept of family. Cinrak had long ago learned to judge Helet's mood by the intake of breath, the length of silence between answers, the heaviness of paw step, or how long she took at morning prayers.

Cinrak was about to explain for the fifth time that only she had permission to land via Mereg's letter of introduction when a thrash of water and a loud cronch erupted. Agnes had found her breakfast. Helet gagged.

Benj smirked at his captain. He'd been far more polite to the matron than she deserved as she fumbled constantly over his name, eventually settling on 'lad' though it sounded bitter on her tongue.

As Cinrak approached the shore, the fairy's shape resolved into something spectacular: big bug-out eyes, impressive crystal-like wings, body and hair woven with flowers and leaves, sharp teeth, and a soft blue glow. According to Mereg's notes, a passel of fairies would be waiting just beyond the treeline for any hint of malfeasance. The recalcitrant fairies were protective

of their land. Many failed Beard expeditions were
noted in bloody detail.

As soon as the sculler crunched onto the sand, the
fairy stepped forward, hand extended.

"Greets. Welcome to Covetona. I am Xit." The fairy
spoke an old dialect without gender signifiers.

They shook, civil style.

"Cinrak the Dapper, o' the *Impolite Fortune*. Pleased
ta be makin' yer acquaintance."

"Aoh. You are folk o' Mereg. They told me about
you." Xit offered a huge closed-mouth smile. A good
sign. "They are good folk. We hope you only takin' the
hair you need, and nothin' else."

Straight to it. The bluntness cheered Cinrak. She
was tired from days of Helet's waffly proclamations
about the Great Mother and heathen spirits.

"Aye, I miss Mereg too. They send me with many
greets. I honour ye an' the land ye allow me ta step
upons." Cinrak gave a little bow, paw to chest. "We
only be takin' o' the Beard what it allows. We be understandin' the volcano be a dangerous place and we only
follow the path ye set for us."

Xit's glow softened further and they swept an arm
in invitation. Cinrak's heavy bones lightened a little as
the fairy led to the way to the Beard. "Aoh. We are
glad you came quick. There is more'n we can harvest
on our own. It is thick growth this season."

"Others follow."

"Aoh. Always the way." Xit blinked those big bug
eyes at the ship resting in the bay, and their smile

crinkled up again at the sight of a frolicking Agnes. "First come, first take. Everyone gets their fair share, includin' the island."

They negotiated time upon the island (not long), numbers of crew (not too many), amount to harvest (just enough), and how far from the Beard they could move (not far). Compared to the lush jungle on either side, the cut's greenery looked only a couple dozen star-turns old. The harvest of the Beard was required so as not to unbalance the life cycle of the jungle. Too little, and the fecundity created by the rotting mass of hair would strangle the fairies' food sources, hamper wildlife, and reduce access to parts of the island. Too much, and the land would lose a vital nutrient source.

"The final things," Cinrak said as she signalled the ship with flags, Agnes gaily mirroring the movements. "First, I be havin' a young 'un eager for their beard. The other—" Cinrak searched for the right words. Best to be blunt. "An old friend wants permission to come ashore. Ye might remember her. Helet."

Xit gave Cinrak a slow once over. Usually that cool vigor would strip her fur right back. But Xit had a *something* about them. Cinrak's capybara chill said: *friend*.

"Aoh. We remember the penitent. Covetona wouldn't let you ashore if they didn't trust you." Xit spoke as if the island was *alive*.

"Ye have me word, as captain, as part o' IRATE, an' as a capybara, that'll I keep 'em in check."

Xit's showed a little more of their sharp teeth. "An' we appreciate it."

The hackles on Cinrak's neck rustled; her salty blood doing its duty. Xit meant more than their fellow fairies when they spoke of the nebulous 'we'. What secrets did Covetona hold close to its magma heart?

THE THUMP OF A book on Cinrak's snout startled her awake. It had only been a moment since she'd put her head down, surely. The laughing calls of the crew, the huff-shick of blades, the wash-hush of the ocean, and warm sand had all blended into a comfortable blanket of sleep.

"Aoh. Cinrak".

She twitched her ears free of sand and blinked up at the sky. How did it get so black and prickled with diamonds?

"Cinrak. We have a problem."

Xit sat cross-legged and cross faced at the bottom of her blanket, their blue glow a cut-out shape in the darkness.

Cinrak snapped fully awake, brushing aside the Great Capybara Mother's words from her dream. Something from the Book of Waters about Her Great Journey had woven around the ocean and the jungle and the glowing, growing face of the mountain, until she had almost touched the words before her.

Her gaze shot to Benj's bed roll and Helet's tent.

"Oh no."

"Oh, yes."

"Steamin' Piles o' Squiddy Poop!" cursed Cinrak. She closed her eyes and scratched her nose. "What ye needin' me to do?"

Xit looked up at the face of the volcano as if searching for inspiration. After a moment, their hair twigs clacked with a single, forceful nod. "Grab your walkin' gear."

"Yer...takin' me. Up there?"

"Nothin' for it. Must find them a'fore...they do too much damage." Xit was already walking towards the dark tree line. "Be quick."

That afternoon, the crew had settled into their work efficiently. Agnes was doing laps around the island, playing with the dolphins, tossing them with her huge tentacles, and making them squee with delight.

Benj had been too excited to stick to one job, so Cinrak let him 'oversee' grading of the hair. She couldn't help but chuckle as he ran between harvesting teams, managing the cuts of perfect length, fondling and sniffing the hair, trying and failing to get it to stick to his face.

Helet had set up a small tent, surrounding herself with books, and strangely stayed silent. When she had turned in from first watch, Cinrak instructed Riddle to keep a keen eye on them both.

A mortified Riddle pulled her patch over her good eye as Cinrak reported the trouble. "I be sorry Cap'n. Thinkin' Benj had finally wound down. An' Helet been so good, if not so good, if ya know what

I mean. Stayin' out from under claw, but not liftin' a paw to help. I enjoyed the moment of glorious peace too well."

"It be fine, friend. When someone be determined, they determined. Jus' keep that tea on the simmer, and your attentions up for the night. If anyone be askin', we went back to the ship. Don't need anyone else gettin' foolish ideas."

The fist of the jungle closed around Cinrak as she joined Xit, humidity squeezing her chest. The fairy paused to communicate with the trees in a low, complicated whistle. After a moment of listening, Xit beckoned her forward into the twisting dark.

"Why you lettin' me in?" Cinrak asked. "Thought ye 'n yers would be able to collect up me wanderers."

"Paths come from many directions and the jungle lets you walk with me awhile," Xit said as they concentrated on their steps.

Cinrak flinched. "I just been readin' something to that effect."

"Aoh?"

"'The intersection o' our paths holds fast our steps an' allows us to carry those who cannot'. Book o' the Waters, chapter five, line seventeen."

"You know your Great Capybara Mother's words." Was that a smirk in Xit's voice? Cinrak couldn't tell through the gloom and glow.

"An' *ye* know them. What do the fairies o' Covetona need with the Mother's words?" A vine caught Cinrak in the face and she slapped it away with a little yelp.

"What do we need with any o' the words o' the world?" Xit spoke light, and Cinrak cursed her ocean-strong lungs. Already she was out of breath from the climb and elevation. "We are curious. We are not cut off like you think us to be. Would be against our best interest not to know the ways o' the world."

As they trudged through the thick jungle, they argued the merits of the common red Mother's primer versus the liberal green and the little known blue used by a conservative splinter faction. After a while, Cinrak realized it was Xit's way of making noise, to alert the jungle and their extended tribe of their passing, and reach the ears of the missing party members without running themselves annoyed and hoarse.

As the moons came up, Cinrak started seeing the minute movements and inhabitants of the jungle. Colourful insects and lizards came out to feed on sap and each other. Leaf litter shivered with slithery things paying the searchers no mind. Birds and small monkeys watched them pass by. Even in the dark there were so many shades of green to enjoy.

Old twinges reminded Cinrak this was the way her ancestors used to live. A lively mountain meant geothermal activity. If there were hot pools higher up, Rodentdom's scientethicalists could speculate capybara life might have grown from here. It made a weird sense for Helet to link the Great Mother to the island.

Thoughts of Helet brought Cinrak down again. Helet had embarrassed her in front of the crew and

Xit. Her guardian had preached against defiance, so it ached Cinrak's bones aplenty Helet didn't practise what she preached.

Xit read the scrunch of Cinrak's furry cheeks. "I understand why Helet be curious. I remember how she spoke of the mountain like it belonged to her. But a scarper seems unlike that young 'un Benj."

"Benj be a good boy, I promisin'." Cinrak peered up at the glow from the mountain's face. "He eager to find a part o' himself. Just hasn't learned growth be patience."

The moss of Xit's eyebrows matted together. "You are using those—" they mumbled to themself and switched to New Fairy. "—words o' gender."

Checking a tree trunk was bitey free, Cinrak leaned and sipped from her canteen. "Aye. The world didn't fit Benj the way he was made, so he makin' himself a man. He be wantin' a beard, and he thinkin' he needs to break off just the right bit o' the mountain."

"Aoh!" Xit said, understanding making their glow shine brighter. "They were one o' yer—" Mumble. "—genders, an' is now another. Fairy nuff."

Cinrak chuckled. Xit made good puns.

Xit continued, "They still broke them rules, though. Up to the mountain what happens, aoh."

Cinrak almost choked on the lukewarm water. The magma better not be thinking of swallowing him up.

They pushed on in silence which grew thick as an oncoming storm, a barely heard rumble beneath her paws.

The night thickened further into a fog, causing Cinrak to watch every step carefully. Everything hurt and each breath tasted of sharp minerals cutting through the loam.

"Uh, Xit? I can't be seein' anything in this fog. Don't ye think we shoulda found 'em by now. Ya know, yer, err, friends, an' everythin'?"

"They be fine."

"Xit! Wait!"

The blue blob bobbed their head. "Ye be lucky. The mountain has called ye."

"A'ight." Cinrak stopped, panting. Even a capybara had limits to their patience. "I bein'...as understandin' as possible. This be...yer land. I only...a visitor, by yer grace. But help me out here. What is it...with ye fairies... an' yer mountain. Like it alive. Like it yer family."

"That be an excellent analogy." A deep voice like rum and charcoal wove out of the fog. "Many paths lead to the mountain, and it is upon us to sit with its wisdom."

Cinrak's ears twitched attempting to locate the speaker. The voice came from everywhere, as if the whole mountain spoke.

"In Her Pawsteps, one-thirteen," Cinrak breathed.

"You know your primer. Good. I had hoped."

A tall, square shape disconnected from the fog, backlit by a hot shimmer from lava vents.

"Great Capybara Mother!" Cinrak stared, eyes wide and filled with stars.

FUR SILVER WITH AGE. Deep dark eyes full of the world's triumphs and misdeeds. An air of danger and strength whirled around the old capybara. Cinrak instinctively knew the elder could take her in a fight.

Xit gave the capybara a simple nod which she returned. Cinrak could almost feel their communication roiling along the medium of silence.

"M...Mother?"

"Oh, you didn't mean it as a curse. Ha! Pssh. Please. Don't get yeself in a twist, me young squiddy." The capybara twirled her paw. "No deities round here. Unless ye count the joy that comes from being close to them best waters in the world."

Something familiar sat within the elder capybara's face, solid stance, and piratical lexicon. Cinrak carefully held out her paw.

"Pleased to be greetin' ya, m'arm. I be Cinrak—"

"—the Dapper, Cap'n o' the IRATE vessel the *Impolite Fortune*, bearer o' the Epics o' stars 'n kraken, an' lover o' the queen an' the diva. Aye, yer reputation preceeds ye." The elder gripped wrists firmly. Her smile made her dark eyes wrinkled with age and mirth almost disappear into her silvering fur. "I be Wautseaster, tender o' water, words, an' hair. An' dun you be m'armin' me, lass. We all the same here."

"There used to be a great pirate named Wautseaster the Fierce." Cinrak tried to take in everything as the elder capybara led them through the fragrant fog, which resolved into...steam! Luxurious geothermal hot pools! "She used to be the mentor o' my mentor, Mereg the Sharp."

"Aye." The elder tossed a bright citrus fruit to Xit. The fairy bit deeply without peeling. "There used to be."

The jungle dwindled and they came out on a wide plateau just beneath the mountain's face scattered with steaming geothermal pools and small pits. A fine house cut out of the rock and a cheery fire licking at a billy of tea finished the homely tableau. Cinrak dipped a paw in a pool scattered with herbs, testing temperature. Perfect.

"Some say she disappeared many star-turns ago in a glorious battle with a shark. Others say she rode a narwhale to the end of the world."

"All could be true." Wautseaster gave a sly wink. "Yet, here I be."

"An' yet others say their old mentor retired quietly with books 'n tea," Cinrak said, finding her smirk. "Aye, Mereg still talks about ye."

"Don't see Mereg as much as I used to. I see a lot o' them in ye. Now yer here, we can secure the next chapter o' the Mothers' way."

Cinrak blinked many times before she could find her words. "Ye be speakin' in the plural."

Mereg's secret. Agnes' insistence they be first to the island. Xit's friendliness. The South Wind's begrudging acceptance of her praise and promises. It all made sense now! A kind conspiracy to get her here.

A new job!

It felt wonderful to be needed.

A familiar voice called from just above their heads. "Cap'n! You made it!"

Benj waved from the lip of the volcano's mouth. There was something bulkier and taller about the lad, as if the mountain had spat out an all new chinchilla.

"Lad! Ye puff powder! Ye ran off without it, ye silly sea snail! This jungle coulda eat ye up without a second bite!"

The beard covered rocks delivered Benj safely with a slip and a slide to the pool plateau. And then Cinrak could see it: Benj had a thick rich beard of the loveliest brown, a wonderful counterpoint to his grey fur.

"I be so angry with ye," Cinrak growled, grabbing him into a fierce hug. "But also glad ye be safe 'n sound. Ye broke the rules! I don't understand. That not be like ye!"

"I had to go, Cap'n. I didn't have time to stop for anything but my coat and boots. It was a silly thing not to tell anyone, but Helet was moving so fast and I didn't want her to get hurt."

Xit nodded approvingly. Benj had only been thinking of someone else's safety, even though Helet had given him so much aggravation. A very piratey thing to do.

Benj continued, "I got turned around. It's so dark in the trees! I walked for ages looking for her and I was getting tired then I realized I didn't know the way back to the beach and the tree trunks were so smooth

I couldn't climb up to find my way and—" he finally paused for breath. "—Wautseaster found me at sunset and brought me here. And hair. Here hair, I mean."

Cinrak held Benj at arm's length, her eyes hot and moist. "An' now look at ye. Yer so handsome."

Cinrak looked to Wautseaster, who was smiling fondly at Benj and smoothing the edge of his beard with a gentle knowing. It took Benj a long time to let other people touch him, and his instant trust in the elder capybara allowed Cinrak to let her suspicions fall away.

"I have my beard." His smile threatened to break his face in two.

"Thank you," Cinrak whispered, letting Benj go to show Xit their beard. The fairy flickered a softer blue and buzzed cross-legged in place, their way to show peace, forgiveness, friendship.

"It be the Mothers' mission to know these things."

"Wautseaster is your grand-mentor!" Benj exclaimed. "Which makes her my great-grand mentor!"

Wautseaster hugged Benj gently. "Aye. That be fer later, when ye feel ye know yerself. Enjoy these early times with yer mind-kin. An' don't think yer getting' off easy with yer flattery. Ye broke Xit's rules. Xit will tell ye what ye need to do to make up for it."

Xit pondered for a moment. "Aoh. We ask you to learn to be an advocate for the fairies."

Benj's eyes were now so round they could almost eat up the stars. "An ambassador? Like the Cap'n to the Felidae? That doesn't sound like a job at all, that sounds like fun!"

"It be a lot o' thankless work. Many people won't like you for it." Xit's glow darkened.

Benj didn't hesitate. "Alright. I'll do it."

"Good. Now go pour yerself a cuppa an' have a dust bath, young 'un." Wautseaster pushed him in the direction of the cheery fire. "The tea will help the weave stick, an' the bath will clean out any critters that be nestin' up in there."

"Wautseaster let me have the *best* hair from Covetona's mouth," Benj said in a dramatic whisper on the way past. He ran his claws through it, face awash with amazement. "I can't wait to show Agnes. She says she can feel it on my face. She likes it! It tingles. Little taps and zaps. Like it's talking to me in code..."

His magic was growing if he could mind-speak to Agnes at this distance. He spoke of his new beard the way Cinrak knew her mer hair rope, brushed with magic from the stars.

Once Benj was out of hearing, Cinrak turned to Wautseaster. "A'ight. Time for ye to talk. What these Mothers ye speak of have to do with the Great Capybara Mother, what they want with me, an apostate by the way, and what they be to do with the Beard? Aye, an' Helet too. Deepest Depths, she still be out there!"

Wautseaster dipped mugs of tea from the large billy, while Benj helped himself from a small one.

She gave a little nod to Xit as she passed him a steaming drink.

"Aoh. She is well. Me fam are keeping her corralled, though she does not know it." Xit sipped their tea, the facets of their big eyes glittering in the firelight. "I will check on her in a moment."

"A little wanderin' in circles will do her good," Wautseaster chuckle-snorted. "It what she best at."

Cinrak breathed through her whirling thoughts. Helet was troublesome, sometimes even on the edge of dangerous to others, but did she deserve punishment like this? She looked from the mysterious old capybara to the fairy for reassurance. They knew their land. They wouldn't let harm come to her. Maybe a little fright at best was all Helet was due.

"Walk with me, lass." Wautseaster beckoned. "We have much to discuss and not much time."

They climbed a well-trod path carving a handsome wrinkle into the chin of the mountain.

"We can never quite predict when the Beard will go into season," Wautseaster said. "We were always expectin' to call ye to the mountain, prob'ly later, with guidance from Mereg. But this be a happy occurrence we took advantage o'."

"I'm to be a guardian o' the mountain, like ye? Like the Great Mother?"

"Aye. And nay. We ask ye to become a guardian o' many things. That be the heart o' the Mothers. We share the load. We ease the burden amongst ourselves, and those of Rodentdom, though they don't know it."

Cinrak paused at the lip of the mouth and took a sip of her tea. A refreshing glow slid right down to her claws.

The width and depth of the cave did nothing to dispel the illusion of mouth-like qualities. Moisture slicked every surface, underlit by a cool green glow. There was a deep scent, of soil and time. Stalactites hung like teeth. Mushrooms poppled the floor like a rough tongue.

From the mushrooms, filaments sprung, rich earthen red, copper, and brown, spreading out from the mouth and down the mountain. The source of the Beard.

"This be just one way we share. The mushrooms taste best fresh, but are just as potent dried an' powdered." Wautseaster plucked mushrooms, examined each, and popped them in a cotton sack. "A little in Benj's tea each day, with honey to taste. Will help the beard take in the early stages, then the rest o' his growth throughout his life. Depending on the way they be brewed the mushroom helps reinforce all sorts o' bodily and mindly things for the likes o' us, with gender an' none. I'll tell ye both which apothecaries be friendly to the Mothers."

The inner cave humidity gave way to the breeze-cut deep night. Wautseaster continued as she showed Cinrak how to brew the tea, then as they stripped off and settled in for a soak. Cinrak could almost hear the creak of her bones as she settled into the hot water.

The Great Mother had not been a deity, simply one capybara or a group of them doing the work of peace, kindness, and goodwill amidst Rodentdom's turbulent ancient times. Now the Mothers were all sorts, and not just capybara. There were those with experience of the care of mind and body. Those with spirituality and none. They moved through all parts of society, bringing perspective and respect.

The Mother's myth worked well to ensure the cooperative continued. The Mothers didn't always agree, and that was their strength. Kindness was an everyday practise, not just a state of being.

Covetona was one place of the Mothers, the fairies happy to do their part to keep the mystery and their autonomy intact. Wautseaster was no leader. The Mothers didn't believe in hierarchal structure; why recreate the power problems of old? A cooperative ensured no one Mother became a target, or if one passed, the whole didn't fall apart. The Mothers met, rested, and moved their Texts all over Rodentdom.

"Movin' the Texts." Cinrak munched an apple plucked from a bowl set beside the pool, a sweet counterpoint to the tea. "Do ye mean to say the Mothers invented piracy?"

"The early Mothers took *advantage*. It helped that pirates were like us, searchin' for a different way to organize. The Mothers worked hard to move away from the plunderin' and lootin' towards a fair distribution of resources ideal."

"IRATE. The union. Another part of the Mothers' plan."

"We don't have a plan. We aim to guide an' support. Put all mammals on equal paws. Leadin' leads to power, an' power leads to imbalance. We lift and sustain. We love equally, to the best o' our abilities."

"'My sister, my love. If she be yer heart, give her ye soul'. Clawsicans, chapter six, line nine. The original Mother was a lesbian, aye?"

"Aye, that be the interpretation. One of the first to stand proud against a vicious slander campaign amongst rodentkind's factions."

"Helet never believed me."

Cinrak sunk down in the water until only the top of her head showed. She blew bubbles through her nostrils.

Secrets upon secrets. Was such a deep secret good for the world? Deities always had a lifespan. Eventually the Mothers would be revealed, maybe not in her lifetime. Feelings would be felt. Accusations of manipulation would be made.

Cinrak rose a little from the water, steam streaming from the slicked fur on her head. "I can't tell Loqui or Orvillia, aye? Or Helet. Ugh. I be no good at lyin'."

"Ye do yer best, an' that be enough." Wautseaster chuckled. "Ha. Mereg can show ye the ways o' better lyin'. They learned from the best."

Cinrak snorted bubbles again. "Oh, aye. So, what do I have to do?"

"Be there for yer fam."

"That's it?"

"Fer now. Oh, an' take up Mereg's old book trade. Books be one of the best weapons in a way of words."

They soaked in companionable silence for a time, until Xit floated back into the clearing. Benj emerged looking fresh, a new man from his dust bath. Cinrak sighed and pulled herself free from the embrace of the hot water.

"We betterin' be fetchin' Helet." Cinrak towelled off. "It must be painin' yer people to have her walkin' on yer land uninvited, Xit."

"We are guidin' her pawfall to be minimal," the fairy shrugged, twig hair rattling. "But, aoh. It is time."

A thought struck Cinrak as she pulled on her work vest, pants, and boots. "Why ye not askin' Helet to be a Mother? Ain't she perfect for the job?"

Wautseaster slipped into pirate work clothes rather than her previous soft robes. "It be a shame, but she don't have the temperament. What she knows about the Great Mother's texts! But her interpretations be too rigid. She not a changin' type."

"Aye," A strange mix of relief and pity warred within Cinrak "She does be lovin' that control."

Wautseaster fetched a tricorner hat and a hip sword. Props. She passed Benj a bag of fresh mushrooms and Xit another orange. "Call me Uster. Just another pirate wantin' a piece o' the beard, an' come to help with the rescue."

"Aye, that be very kind o' ye, Cap'n Uster." Cinrak saluted.

With one last long gaze upon the plateau, Cinrak and Benj said their silent farewells to the peaceful place. For the time being.

"What if I'd said nay to the job?" Cinrak asked as the jungle took them in its embrace once more.

A sly smile reminiscent of Mereg cut Wautseaster's furry silver face. "We choose so well no one says nay."

Cinrak swallowed her argument.

"Now, ship hierarchy," Wautseaster said, warm voice weaving with the dark. "Somethin' I'd been workin' on with Mereg..."

As Cinrak let her new friend ramble on, the North Wind brushed her ears with promises of a fair ride towards home.

Towards her new challenge.

CETACEOUS SECRETS OF THE JEWELLED NADIR

Tail the Sixth:
In Which a Mysterious Whale Takes Our Captain to Their Fall

"**A**GNES WANTS US TO what an' where now?"

The riggings of the *Impolite Fortune* went as taut as an unplucked string, and the ocean all around went so silent it was almost as if the water was holding its breath.

"She wants us to follow Xolotli to Whale Fall," Benj the chinchilla said, slow and careful. The tips of Agnes the kraken's giant orange tentacles wriggled above water off starboard, as if narrating the behest by kraken sign language. "Xolotli has something they want to share with you, Cap'n."

Cinrak the Dapper, capybara captain of the pirate vessel *Impolite Fortune*, sucked her underbite bottom lip with her large upper front teeth. Oh, she did love a good mystery of the ocean deep, and Xolotli, Agnes' glass whale lover and denizen of the Edge of the World, was the most mysterious of them all. But sometimes her fame as adventurer, most visible member of the

137

International Rodent Aquatic Trade Entente, friend to the Felidae, and member of the secret capybara Mothers' cabal rested heavy on her shoulders. Secrets could break anchors, friendships, and hearts if not tended well, and Cinrak tended many.

"Not be like Xolotli to share anythin'. So when the glass whale asks, we do."

Her first mate, Riddle, sidled up, ratty whiskers taut. "What be Whale Fall, ser?"

"It be where whales go to die." Cinrak tried and failed to imagine the enormous graveyard. "Somewhere so deep their bones rest an' their flesh becomes one with the water."

Riddle's patchwork face fur twitched in horror. "Be Xolotli dyin'?"

"Benj? Agnes' ain't losing her love so soon after findin' them? That'd be terrible!"

"Nay, Cap'n. Agnes says they're almost as long-lived as she is. This be a—" the chinchilla scrunched up his fluffy silver brow and stared at his large crus-taceous friend. "—journey downward we must trust in. That's the best translation I can manage."

Riddle switched their eye patch to their good eye with a groan. "We ain't goin' down another whirly-pool, eh?"

Agnes' tentacles wriggled, pointing west.

"No. We'll be following...the border."

"But Agnes says there be no borders in the ocean!"

"Hmm, that didn't translate right." Benj took on too serious a mien for a youngfur. "We'll be following a pilgrimage...?"

Riddle danced from paw to paw. She liked big things, she couldn't lie, but only above water where she could control them.

Cinrak judged the angle of the sun, the happy scud of clouds, counted the moon dance, and came to a conclusion. "It be the Partin', innit?"

The entire crew gasped so loud a breeze brushed up close thinking it was a courting ritual. The ocean slapped the side of the vessel in applause. The riggings creaked as the masts craned in the direction Agnes pointed.

Benj's eyes went very round. "Aye. Agnes' says that's the right name for it."

"Cap'n!" Riddle spun. "That be the tide o' all tides. Some say strange magics be afloat. The moons ain't friendly then! No one ever seen the whales' graveyard a'tween the walls o' water out deep when the Partin' at full strength."

Cinrak straightened her bow tie. "Aye, Riddle me friend. Maybe we'll be the first."

Riddle groaned. "If there could be *anythin'* worse than a whirly-pool to quiver yer liver an' drown ye in sorrow, it be the Partin' o' the Waves an' masses o' whale bones!"

Cinrak signalled to the crew. "Go west, me friends! We have dead whales to find!"

"SKITTERING BABY SEAHORSES!"

Columbia, perched on the mid rail, paused mid brush of a red tress, staring at Cinrak with mouth open and eyes wide. His moustache quivered and iridescent tail fins flicked.

"Ye could've dumped all the squiddy poo in the ocean on me head an' I wouldn't've been more surprised." Cinrak paced the deck, forepaws behind her back, wind ruffling her fur. The *Impolite Fortune* loved having the wind at at its back and maintained a fair clip to keep up with the converging whale pods.

"The mer have never been invited to Whale Fall! I am most excited for you. Do you think they'll let me tag along?" Columbia's winter-grey eyes surrounded by orange scales went very wide.

"I'll get Benj to ask Agnes. But it be hard to get anythin' outta her. She dancin' like a wee babby squid." She twisted her forepaws in loose approximation of the kraken's excitement.

Columbia's face relaxed into round-cheeked sweetness. "All that beautiful death."

"Columbia!" Cinrak snapped her claws, and the mer shook himself, sharing a sharp-tooth grin. "Help me out here. Ye've ridden the Partin' before. Tell me what I'm suppose to do!"

"Ridden it, yes. But only the very edges, and not all the way to the end. The walls get too turgid and steep." Columbia drew an air-picture with his hairbrush. "And there's no telling whether a fin, a two- or four-leg could take to the seabed before the walls come crashing in. It might be like the Void at the Edge of the World, or completely different."

"So how'm I s'posed to enter Whale Fall without bein' crushed to death or drownin'? What Xolotli be thinkin'?"

"Who knows what any glass whale thinks?" Columbia's shrug looked like a dance move. "They're not fond of interacting with rodent or merkind."

Riddle joined the conversation with a salute, paw to breastbone. "Thirteen knots, ser, an' barely keepin' up with the whales. Good thing the nor'easter came to play."

"Hang in there, me lovely." Cinrak patted the railing. The riggings creaked their promise and the sails snapped at each other to pay attention.

"How long we gotta keep this up?" Riddle glanced nervously at the huge shadows barging along all around. "The crew be full o' spark, an' the weather be good, but when we get near that Partin' —"

"—It'll be like ridin' a wave ye can't even dream of," Cinrak finished. "I ken. Xolotli promises we'll be safe. Break out the good fruit, and make sure there be an extra helpin' for lunch." She raised her voice. "Hey ho! Ye all be doin' the star's work!"

The crew hey ho'd back and cheered. Riddle strode away, twirling her tail in anticipation of a good meal.

Columbia resumed brushing, allowing Cinrak to gather up stray hairs. "Where is the young merfur?"

Cinrak quick-checked deck stations. "Ain't seen Benj in a while. He keepin' watch on Agnes, I s'pect."

"And just *how* does he do that? Travel with Agnes, I mean. Keep dry. Keep from getting all fungused up in that chinchilla way."

Cinrak blinked. "Ya know, I don't be knowin'. They get where they need to be. Not for me to interfere. He be havin' regular dust bath, an' he carry puff powder at all times. Just so long as he stays dry, it's all good."

All at once, the undercurrent of whale song that had followed them all sun rose to quite the ache of a cetaceous choir. Cinrak checked the cloudless sky: yes, all the moons had fled, chasing each other in some ancient grudge they wouldn't let mammals solve for them.

The high watch called an "Ahoy!" and a fearful sound rose from the ocean like many tentacle suckers letting go of solid air.

Woven with orange flashes, a huge wave humped far off to starboard. The wall of water kept going up and up, and the crew hauled the ropes to turn the ship to safety. Agnes burst through the surface, tentacles flailing like she was about to take flight. Whale tails flicked and the huge shadows surged ahead.

When the wall hit an unsustainable angle, Agnes wheeled through the air and crashed to the surface below.

Everyone on board got thoroughly soaked, except Columbia who always maintained a sensible damp sheen and glamorous glimmer.

Then Benj was there, clambering over the starboard rail, panting, grinning, and very dry.

"The Parting has started, ser!" He smacked off a salute. "Xolotli needs you to come now!"

Cinrak slicked her claws across her ears, flicking off excess water. "We gotta get away from that there wave. It be huge!"

"Don't worry, ser!" Benj danced around, winding his beard tip in imitation of Columbia. "Xolotli promises some whales will keep the Parting in check so the ship won't be swamped."

"Ya mean it could be bigger?" Riddle shrieked, claws turning grey from the grip she had on the wheel. "Fartin' Puffer Fish an' all the Tail's Glory, this gonna be one for the ages!" She settled her eye patch in place and lashed her tail to the wheel. "Ye get goin' Cap'n. This one's a'tween me, the ocean, an' big whale butts! Ha!"

Cinrak chewed her whiskers as she stripped off her boots. There was no way her little sculler could survive that monster wave, let alone her swimming in it. If she was to walk along the seabed, how was she to get over the wall?

Rising from the deep, the glass whale came.

Heart pumping, lungs pushing, stomach churning, silver-blue blood moving. Their jewel-like organs could all be seen through translucent flesh as Xolotli gently breached. They blew a mist of water in greeting, soaking Cinrak all over again.

Benj waved to the whale, grin plastered on his face. "All aboard!"

"Aye?" Cinrak couldn't help but smile. A notoriously shy glass whale letting itself be seen above water was a sight to behold. Agnes swam delicately around her love, tentacles framing their magnificence.

"Xolotli is inviting you to climb aboard."

"Where? How?"

Creeeeaaaak.

Xolotli's mouth hinged wide. A long pink tongue extended.

Cinrak stared. "In...there?"

"In there."

Down the maw of the beast.

Fur quivering, Cinrak said, "Aye, I came to sea to see some wild things. Add one more to me Epic. Just so long as they ain't gonna digest me in long slow agony an' poop me out the other end."

"You won't be eaten," Benj laughed. "Agnes promises."

"An' Xolotli?"

"That's their promise."

"Translated."

"Aye."

Nothing for it, if she was to prove her gumption to the crew and add her name to an Epic.

She stepped over the large, sharp teeth onto Xolotli's tongue, which squished spongier than mouldy bread. The tongue stayed extended and the teeth did not chomp her in half.

Feeling very alone, she turned and called. "Benj?"

Nothing.

"Columbia?"

A gush of water. She peered into the dying light. A flash of red and orange, scales shimmering, hair swirling.

"Columbia!"

The mer pushed his hair out of his face as he flopped upright. "How undignified. But still, I've been invited!"

"Marvellous!"

"Darling, you have no idea. Xolotli apparently wants to honour my contribution at the Edge of the World. I tried to tell them via Benj it's just what mer do. But, well. Who could resist the likes of divine me?"

A shaky chuckle escaped Cinrak. It felt good not to be alone. "Shall we?"

"Is there any other way in?"

Columbia swam along the stream provided while Cinrak lurched along the soft tongue. All light faded, her back paws slipped, and the only way was down.

The complete dark ate her shriek.

With a damp squish, she landed somewhere soft and warm.

"Columbia?"

No reply.

"Xolotli?" She hated how her voice quivered.

A pulse of light, above and to her right.

"Can you understand me?"

The light pulsed twice.

"Where's Columbia? Where am I? Am I going to drown? Or dissolve in your juices?"

The light flourished, dimmed, flourished again, held. She was encased in a sac just big enough to stand and hold her arms out in all directions. The enormous valves of Xolotli's heart fluttered nearby. Receding into the dark were other structures of blue, pink, and red. On the other side of the heart, another sac, holding a fascinated Columbia like a goldfish in a bowl. Cinrak waved and called, but the mer didn't acknowledge her presence. But he was alive, and that's what mattered.

"How can I breathe in here?" A ponderance with no explanation, though the implications were enormous. Glass whales had *evolved* to carry air-breathing life inside!

Little feeling of Xolotli's movements translated through the whale's translucence, just wispy water and shadowed shapes. Cinrak peered between the whale's iridescent ribs. What a show! Her heartbeat calmed, and a sense of quiet joy smoothed over her fur.

The uncontained beauty of the deepest depths opened up for her.

Tiny stars flickered around Xolotli's body, reminding Cinrak of the lights that had made up the whale's home, the upside down ocean-sky at the Edge of the World. Were these lights creatures living in parasitic comfort, or shreds of magic?

Xolotli burst through a wall of water.

Cinrak fell back. Such might and speed!

And now they...floated. In the air. Just above the drying sea-bed.

This. This was the Parting.

Xolotli's stars glittered in the muted sunlight. Two great, smooth walls of water encased a path of the exposed sea-bed leading back for at least two clicks, crashing in behind the last of the whale pilgrims. Even encased in whale flesh, Cinrak could smell the distance and ferocity with her salty weather sense.

And in front...

Xolotli undulated near the head of the pod, allowing Cinrak to see whales of all types churning, turning, and surging in delight at the moonless air on their flesh. More sparkles rose from them, stars heading for the stars, brushing the walls of water, stitching them tightly in place.

In the opposite sac, a beatific expression smoothed Columbia's bearded face younger than his many star-turns, and his tail scales shone brighter than Cinrak had ever seen them.

Cinrak ran her forepaws down her broad cheeks and barrel chest. Maybe the depths compressed her, or that magic light played tricks, but her fur felt younger too, lighter.

After forever and no time at all, the whales circled up, dashing back and forth to help the lights keep the water walls stable.

Whale Fall had been reached.

Cinrak leaned forward, heart so full she thought she was going to spill its contents through Xolotli and they'd become a marvellous merger of capybara and whale. The sea-bed field widened as the whales floated in increasing circles. A group were doing a fine job of shunting fish away before the water completely disappeared.

A world of hidden treasures spread out beneath her paws in the whale graveyard.

Xolotli took their time, showing Cinrak everything: bright white and iridescent whale skeletons in repose, as if they would swim up to join their siblings once rested; an antique, broken, and barnacled ship, enjoying its rest as crabs kept it company; rocks shining obsidian, the sand like fool's gold.

And jewels. So many of them. Dotting the sea-bed, the compressed organs of whales passed. Xolotli dipped closer for Cinrak to truly appreciate the superb sapphires, rubies, emeralds, and diamonds.

Reminded of the Heart of the Ocean Xolotli had gifted her, Cinrak's paws twitched. It still lay in secret, locked away in the kraken-sprite protected chest, waiting for the right home. Which, as it turned out, was not the queen's crown.

Xolotli dipped lower, belly almost brushing the sand.

Cinrak gasped.

A memory from her life played out in each of the jewels littering the graveyard. The glittering, the cracked, the dust. The treasure trove of her life.

Her ears twitched. It must be monumental imagination brought on by Depth's Sickness.

But no. There her memories and worries were. Orvillia and Loquolchi. Mereg, Benj, the Mothers' collective. Her ship, crew, and the union. Holding rodentkind and the Felidae together. The orphanage and her past. All lifted gently from her and allowed to rest on the sea floor, held safe within the embrace of the ocean.

The salt and stars polished the jewels, and the ocean-sky medium tumbled them to show all their facets. The completedness of her. And all that she could be.

Her thoughts stopped churning like tide foam. Once more that lightness of her fur, as if turned inside out, refreshed and reworn like her favourite tailored suit. Her body felt as light as the air passing through the whale's lungs.

She was the Capybara.

She could stay like this forever.

Xolotli undulated through the ocean-sky void just as easily as they did the water. The lights, the stars... maybe there were the spirit of countless whale generations — those been, gone, and forever — holding space for hearts and souls to mend.

All the whales moved in practised fashion, taking turns to maintain the split in the ocean, dancing around each other, reacquainting themselves with old friends, clicking and harping songs of their time apart. The whales' wails were sharp in the magical medium unlike the way they carried in water. Another honour to be held so close, secrets only shared by the few, the great, the humble, the magnificent. The longer she listened, the more she thought she could almost understand what they were saying, then another wonder would catch her eye and she would lose the thread of the idea.

A great skeleton loomed close, and she wondered dreamily if they were about to be swallowed again. Capybara within whale within whale.

Xolotli slid between the ribs with a tenderness Cinrak could only hope to achieve with her loves, settling their head into the great skull, great hump against spine. Did they ask the ghost what it was thinking, transfer its memories into their body? Xolotli's light pulsed, and they lifted away from the bed, the encasing skeleton snug about their limpid flesh.

Their flight took them towards the water wall. Noooooo...so soon?

Had she said that aloud? Was that what her voice sounded like? Nowhere deep and long as whale song, but a resonance that carried authority and love.

The water. Abyssal black. Thick, unctuous. Home encasing home. Encasing her. Liquid arms rocking her gently, until there was nothing left but flesh and fur, heartbeat and breath.

A name. Someone was calling a name. C-k c-k. A whale click? She was the whale. Ocean smoothing her flesh, flesh swallowing the ocean whole.

THE DECK OF THE *Impolite Fortune* held its captain with welcome regard. Cinrak lay still, letting the sun warm her. Salt crusted her fur, vest and pants tightening as they dried. It didn't matter. Nothing mattered. She was here.

Voices mumbled and sighed in that staccato way of air breathing mammals. The sails above her hung at ease, caressing the breeze clear of rushing and roaring. The ship beneath her moved with elegant persuasion.

Solicitous paws helped her stand. She pushed them away gently. The old instincts, her sea legs, were still there. Always there. Her salt. Her lifeblood.

Cinrak's reality returned in full with the bittersweet tingles of memory and careful worries.

"How is Xolotli?" Cinrak leaned on the rail.

"They're fine, ser." Benj pointed to the playing pod. Agnes swam excited rings about the whale who hovered just below the surface. The *Impolite Fortune* rocked gently in their wake, safe in their watery arm. "More to the point, how are you?"

The wash of images tumbling together made her pull back on her words.

"I don't know. Xolotli showed me wonders that be not mine to share."

Benj's eyes glazed. "Agnes says it's alright for you to talk about the what, just not the how."

Cinrak chuckled. "I don't be knowin' the how. An' I sure don't know a heck of a lot of the what, either."

Columbia's laugh tinkled like the first pops of stars at twilight. He perched in his favourite position on the rail, plaiting his beard, tail jiggling. "That's alright then. I'm not going belly up. I'm not sure what I saw either, but it was *lovely*. I'm honoured the whales chose to share with me."

The crew all crammed along the rail, gushing over the glass whale. So pretty!

"Lookit what Xolotli be wearin'," Cinrak said. "Them bones an ancestor mebbe, or a friend. It looks like..."

"Armour," Columbia murmured.

"They be findin' a way to interact with our world."

"Dear Xolotli. So shy. So sweet."

Cinrak groomed the salt from her fur to hide her warm cheeks. Something so large feeling vulnerable to the perception of mammals they had to wear a disguise? Cinrak wanted to hold them tight, but her embrace was so small compared to Xolotli and their life in the Infinite Void.

She put a gentle forepaw on her Benj's shoulder. "Thankee for yer help there. Yer a good lad, Benj. I proud o' ye."

Benj quick-groomed his beard, a tell against his embarrassment. "You say that all the time, Cap'n."

"Nay. Not enough. I be making up for all the times I didn't hear it as a lass."

Benj stared at her, forehead fur scrunched up. No matter that he didn't understand now.

The glass whale blew a fine mist that fell like diamonds around the crew. They shrieked and laughed in delight, wiping the sheen off their fur and quills.

"D'ya think ye could pinpoint Whale Fall on a map, Cap'n?" Riddle ran her tail through her forepaws. Sometimes Cinrak couldn't take the old pirate ways out of her first mate.

Cinrak shared a look with Columbia. His eyes and beard glistened with more than his usual dampness. A promise passed along the silence between them. She still carried many things, but she could see how to balance them better.

Cinrak might never enter Whale Fall again, but if her salty balance adjusted by being near the graveyard for a time, then it would be a boon to her soul.

"Nay," Cinrak sighed, resting her chin in her paws. "That be a'tween them whales an' the ocean."

This was a secret that would be no burden at all.

FLIGHT OF THE HYDRO CHORUS

Tail the Seventh:
In Which Our Hero Discovers
Unknown Depths to the Stars

ON A TINY ISLET far to the west in the Felidae archipelago, Cinrak lay in the sand, wriggling in its coarse finery to attend itches of vague guilt.

The sun threw its last warm arms around the shoulders of the Paper and Moth moons to help balance the weight between dark and night. The sky coruscated through lavender to cetacean blue to velvet violet, with citrus and silver lacing the edges.

This Aestivus equinox race for the stars would be different. No rat courtiers cutting their eyes at a pirate's presence, no over excited fairies, no dancing cats, no devious plans or demands. Just her capybara body, a mer hair rope, and a salty song lifted into the sky, searching for the answer to a change in the constellations.

Searching for grain of truth in a legend.

"It's dangerous to go alone," came a voice above and beyond the tideline. "Take us."

In one final dramatic flourish, the sun had thrown out burnt orange arms as if to say "All stars welcome to the night stage, Cinrak the Dapper, our favourite capybara pirate!".

Balanced at the tip of one of these arms was a chinchilla-shaped silvery glow.

The glow burst with a 'pwop'. The sun beam wriggled and lowered the passenger with a reverence only a giant kraken could reserve for her mind-kin.

A-Benj the Ocean Star hop stepped onto the sand from Agnes' outstretched tentacle.

"Benj me lad!" A little healthy fear strangled a surprised croak from Cinrak. She clasped her cabin kit's wrist pirate-style. "That be spectacularly tentacular."

"Agnes loves to make an entrance." Benj combed claws through his blooming brunette beard. The tea made from mushrooms of the Covetona volcano was doing wonders for his transition. "Our little secret. It's how I get around the ocean with her without drowning or dying from wetness. And it's how we'll meet the stars without running out of breath for the Song."

"I be honoured she and ye be wantin' to share." Cinrak gave a deep bow in the direction of the lagoon. Agnes waved a tentacle tip back. "But I be unsure o' what ye mean, goin' alone. Goin' where?"

"Oh, Cap'n, my Cap'n. The equinox ride calls to all those made of stars. You're not going without me and Agnes. And we wouldn't go without you."

A crackle-hiss raced across the clear sky. The two turned towards the whispering waves of a different type of ocean, one that swept beyond their earthly knowns. The first overeager stars were hitting the upper reaches, breaking apart in fine showers of fire and dust to feed excited mammal eyes and gaping fish mouths.

The mer hair coiled at Cinrak's hip sent a staticky buzz through her fur, and she soothed the rope with soft strokes. A useful instrument since she had used it to rein in a star on that first wild ride, it had started twitching a portent some tri-tides back.

"The stars haven't forgotten the good you did for them. Neither has Agnes."

Benj pulled celestial charts from inside his thick black buckle-neck jacket, a sartorial choice that filled the pool of pride in Cinrak's chest.

He pointed at a constellation on the chart, then at its matching shape in the sky. Or somewhat matching; the one in the sky was much brighter, elongated, and closer than the old drawing.

"The Eight Sisters," Cinrak pulled on the hem of her best tailored jacket, all purple paisley highlights offset by a green silk bow tie. "Ya guessed tha same as me how they'd point the way to the changin' tides."

"Not a guess. Good research. All that time spent in the Merholme libraries paid off. You put together the puzzle pieces left by astronomicalers, how the Eight Sisters approached and receded quicker than most other celestial bodies. I needed to match what Agnes could share of the blood memory her siblings left for her in the egg, how they were the arrow pointing in the direction the kraken went."

"I be glad yer here, truly. I was wrong to keep this all for meself." Cinrak patted Benj's shoulder.

A little of the old boyish sweetness peeked out in his grin. "I think I understand. You were trying to protect us from disappointment, like a good captain does. But you can count on me. I've become so strong!" He flexed his little chinchilla arms.

"But we don't have much time. I ken something be agitatin' Agnes lately. Oh, aye. I can't taste her with me salt, her magic be way too strong, but I see how her colour be deepened, how she floats at night with that great eye turned up." The kraken waved from the dolphin pile it was tickling to delighted squeals around the reef. "If mah readin's be right, we be in need of a special song to sing up them depths. 'Cept I ain't a singer and what song do ye sing when ye have no breath up there? An' as far as I ken, a kraken don't be havin' a voice box to speak of."

"That's where you need me." A third voice startled the three out of their collusion. Wood hush-crunched against wet sand behind them. "If I was to guess from my readings of the myths, Agnes lost her voice with her siblings."

"Hello, Mum." Benj planted a big kiss on Loquolchi the marmot diva's black and grey furry cheek as he helped her out of the sculler.

She brushed him off with a laugh. "Told you not to call me that. Makes me sound old. A diva never grows old."

Cinrak had the temerity to look abashed, whiskers twitching. "I thought ye were celebrating equinox wit Orvy an' the Felidae."

"It's our anniversary! I'm not going to celebrate without you!" Loquolchi studied the sky like she would study jewellery. A streak of fire cut it in two. "I've arrived just in time, it seems. Just as well. Neither of you can hold a tune to save your lives."

Cinrak squeezed her love to her barrel chest. "I wouldn't exactly call this celebrating. 'Sides, seems ta me ya have flyin' on yer mind."

Loquolchi peeked sweetly sideways through her lashes. "Whatever gives you that idea?"

"Yer here. Snuck up on me quite talented, must be sayin'. Congratulations on yer piratey skills, ya salty wee troubadour. An' ya've pulled the Moth moon silk dress outta storage."

"Happy to be guilty as charged on all counts," Loquolchi simpered, swirling the sensational silk still silvery after all these star-turns. It whispered about Loquolchi's ankles in anticipation of taking to the sky, and the coil of mer hair rope at Cinrak's hip whispered back a low harmony.

Another crack of star meeting air, and Cinrak involuntarily took a step towards the tideline.

Loquolchi pulled her back, stronger than her soft energy gave off.

"Have you really thought this through?" she demanded. "Letting the stars take you on a flight over uncharted waters. You could drown! Or die from the fall alone!"

Cinrak caressed her face with a soft paw. "If a pirate don't trust the ocean to keep her well, then she be no pirate at all. And I be trustin' them stars. They be...needin' me. As much as the ocean."

"Cat litter!" Loquolchi stomped a rearpaw. "Me and Orvy need you alive more!"

"I couldn't live with meself if I didn't do something to help Agnes. She has us, but she alone too, and we know that shouldn't be the case. Creatures we only know from myths aren't so myth-like anymore, all disrupting things. Now we know it be the kraken's job to keep them in balance. Agnes can't do it all on her own."

"I believe you. Orvy believes you. Anyone who knows the ocean even an ounce the way you do believes something is off out there."

"Cap'n," Benj murmured, looking from a chart to the sky. "We have to go."

"But how? We can't breathe that far up." Loquolchi cringed away from the wavelets lapping at her claws.

"We won't be riding a star. Except—" Benj tilted his fuzzy head side to side. " — in a way, we will be. It's too hard to explain. It's best we just show you."

The kraken's spade-shaped head popped up and her single enormous eye regarded her land-based friends with unreadable depths, woven with the seas of time she had swum through.

Benj gestured and Agnes reached out a tentacle. The tip sparkled as if the sun struck water drops, reminding Cinrak of the luminescence of Whale Fall. The light grew into a perfect orb in synchronicity with Agnes' fluttering gills.

Benj stepped up onto the tip of the tentacle and into the gleaming orb, his fur taking on a delicious glow. He extended a forepaw. "Welcome aboard the Agnes Express."

"If the kraken were out there all this time, where those sisters are pointing," Loquolchi stalled, gesturing towards the horizon. "Why didn't Agnes just go looking for them?"

"Because they didn't want to be found." Benj stroked the kraken's skin. Agnes shivered with delight, the love evident in the brightening of the sphere. "They had something that needed to be done beyond our ken."

"But they left poor Agnes all alone!"

Benj gave a sad little smile. "She has her whale family. She has Xolotli. We have each other. She has the whole ocean. That was enough. Until the tides turned. She's been having to battle the creatures of the deep increasingly more these last few star-turns. She doesn't like that." Agnes' great flesh trembled for a moment, and the glowing orb dimmed. "She only hunts for food and those monsters taste dreadful apparently."

Water bubbled and popped at Agnes' rear. The kraken raised a few more tentacles above water. Irritation at delay? A shrug? Apology?

Cinrak had touched Agnes' skin before — a shoulder tap here, a thank-ye pat there — but never had she *stood* upon the kraken. Rather than rubbery and slick, her skin had a coarse quality that helped Cinrak stay in place. The same tingle that wove through the mer hair coursed along Agnes. Agnes was older than any living being and had seen so much, yet she contained an exuberance, sweetness, and passion for people that went beyond measure.

She was, Cinrak decided, the best of them all.

Benj gripping his mothers' paws tightly was the only warning. Cinrak's breath was swept away as they rushed away from land.

Belying her earlier reticence, Loquolchi had plenty of breath. She shoved it into a shriek that went through two octaves, then settled into a squealing laugh. "ImgoingtodiebutIdontcarrrrrrrrre!"

Spreading her forepaws wide, to reveal the majesty of the Moth moon silk dress, she stepped to the tip of Agnes' outstretched tentacle and burst into the soprano's lead aria 'Ever Bright, The Shining Falls' from *The Legion Sky*.

The pull of the ocean still having a hold on her, Cinrak quickly slung her rope around and under Agnes' tentacle and tied it about her waist. Benj stood at ease, though he did not look down.

Cinrak pressed her paws firm against the slight stick of Agnes' skin as the tentacle wove this way and that, negotiating oncoming young stars.

"Deepest Depths!" Cinrak finally found enough breath to speak. She adjusted her volume as she discovered she didn't have to battle the wind for airspace, only Loquolchi. "Them mythmakers got a lot to answer for, not listenin' proper to the sea folk."

Benj blew out a long hard breath, like there were things he needed to forget. People always underestimated his size. "We practised before this, during other equinoxes. She can only rise up when the pull of the ocean is less than the pull of the stars."

"When her siblin's song is strongest."

"Aye. When the constellation of the Eight Sisters swings closest." Benj's gaze stayed true to the largest stars of all.

In that moment it all became *real* for Cinrak. What Benj and the myths said about krakens and mer.

"They not be pointin' the way. They not be stars at all. The Eight Sisters are the kraken." She drew a length of the mer hair rope through her claws. Now it was fair sizzling, and her fur stood on end.

"There is much we don't know about our ocean siblings, but one thing is true," Benj said. "They were born of stardust."

Only a dull roar came from outside, the air fresh and easily breathable within. Agnes' bubble must have properties Rodentdom's scientheticals would start wars to research. Cinrak had told Benj she would do everything in her power to make sure that didn't happen. It would take a cunning mix of subterfuge and truth sewn within Rodentdom's storytellers to keep Benj and Agnes free and safe. Just the sort of use of half-truths they were railing against. Truth belonged to safety, not to maintaining hierarchies of power.

Agnes reached up and up, the darkness intensifying. The stars' gaze stayed steady upon them. The Eight Sisters loomed large, their sparkling arms solidifying into something more than light.

The three moons delighted in their intricate dance. Cinrak had never seen the Silver Moon this large or bright; it showed its shy face at unusual times. With the curtain of earthly light pulled aside, she could see easily how its face swirled with its strange clouds.

Cinrak risked a quick peek over the edge, and immediately regretted it. Their trajectory had taken them far out over the Unknown Ocean, an onyx mirror reflecting only the boldest lights.

The boom and crackle of the stars pitched through the muffle of the bubble. Agnes wove between the bright threads with ease, making Cinrak's heart claw at her breast bone. How did Agnes manage to breathe? She seemed in her element.

Loquolchi cut off mid warble. "You're not paying attention!"

"Apologizin', m'love. Takes some o' us a moment to adjust to"—Cinrak had to wet her mouth to continue—"bein' up this high." She scooted on her bottom towards the narrow large tip of the tentacle. "Yer singin' be beautiful, though."

"It's not just about beauty." Loquolchi stomped her rearpaw and Agnes' orange flesh barely shivered. "It's *necessary*! If we want to attract the stars', erm, the kraken's attention, we need to give them good reason to come back down!"

Benj looked helplessly between his chosen mothers. "Agnes can talk to her siblings by mind speak, but you're right, Loquolchi, about her losing her voice. It's been so long and they've seen so much, their language has probably drifted. Even the way Agnes speaks has changed in the long time she's lived with the whales. It's a matter of finding a point of recognition, even a small spark of sound."

"I be partial to 'The Ballad o' the *Lavender Menace*' meself," Cinrak muttered, annoyed the other two could balance *and* talk at the same time. "That be loud in the later verses."

"You would, wandering heart." Loquolchi pinched Cinrak's cheek. "You might think you've been very clever with your research and deep thoughts, but did it ever occur to you *I* might know a little about star song?"

The air bubble pulsed, and Benj nodded.

"'The Legion Sky' isn't a passing fancy. I have made it my life's joy to know the history of this mer penned opera. It's hundreds of star-turns old and is updated every few decades. It is a living story, a rule of its composers passed down through generations."

Loquolchi paced the length of the bubble as if she was simply giving a lecture to theatre apprentices. "Alas, Rodentdom's opera aficionados have become a little stuffy in the last three score star-turns or so, and have not truly experienced it in the medium it was originally designed to be performed in." Her silk wings swished as she gestured down. "Under water! Ah, but Loquolchi, you say. We are in a medium much thinner than water. Sound doesn't carry at higher altitude."

She was really into this now. Even Agnes seemed into the lecture, the bubble pulsing as the kraken turned and levelled out into the middle of the celestial pack, keeping pace with the irrefragable stars.

"But here's the drop that gets lost in the ocean." Loquolchi whirled. Behind her, the leading Sister of the Eight seemed to balance on the tip of Agnes' outstretched tentacle. "Certain early versions of the opera were created to be performed atop mountains, lyrics adjusted to call to the sky. And *that,* my darling creatures, is why you need me!"

With a final flourish of her voluminous skirts, Loquolchi continued to sing from the note where she left off.

Benj and Cinrak stared, stunned.

"Do ye ken the opera well?" Cinrak asked out of the corner of her mouth.

Benj screwed up his face. "My mother made me learn the alto parts as a kit. But since my voice has dropped, I've learned the tenor and bass parts too."

"I ken the love song."

"Of course you do," Benj smiled.

"And Agnes?"

"She has heard the underwater version multiple times. Enjoys it very much."

"But I also mean—" Cinrak circled a paw at the bubble, the constellation, the stars now so close they were throwing off sparks. "—alla this. Did she *ken* that now be the right time to fly high and fast?"

"I'm embarrassed to admit that I thought her size would be her downfall." Benj stroked the tentacle and it wiggled just a little. Cinrak gripped her lasso tighter. "She says...in all the star-turns she has...waved...yes that's the best I can translate...waved to the sky, this is the strongest, err, *pull*, she has ever felt from the Eight Sisters. Her siblings."

"Goes against everythin' we ken of our wordly physics, but fer now we run with it." Cinrak wound the tail ends of the mer hair rope around her paws. "Doesn't need to make sense now. We analyse later."

"We're out of time, my dears," Loquolchi sing-songed, pointing at the constellation. It now had shimmer, fire, and form, their many points writhing like tentacles. "'Dance of the Eight Spears' on my count. One two three four..."

More pirate than performer, Cinrak hummed the melody and bleated the words she knew, having heard Loquolchi practice and perform the opera often.

What would the kraken look like after nearly a thousand star-turns wandering beyond the limits of mammal understanding? Surely Agnes would gather their notice, but she had been here before, to no avail.

Agnes honed in on the Eight Sisters, her tenacious spirit shining through from the bubble and orange flesh taut with anticipation and effort.

Cinrak tried to reach out with her ocean sense, but she could only taste the way ice and wind brushed against land and ocean. There was a tang of salt buried in the elements surrounding the Eight Sisters, the bubble of life that kept them alive in the airless empyrean, but she could not penetrate deeper. Needing all her senses to stay balanced, she pulled back and concentrated on what she could control—singing to the kraken-stars, convincing them they were needed to rebalance the oceans and their family.

Running stars crashed and burned against each other, taking turns to dip low enough to graze their underbellies against the air, sending up sparks, whipping and moving to the beat of the sky only they could understand, the great breath of life.

Now the stronger stars were pulling back, having tasted enough of the air-filled world for another star-turn.

Little quivers coursed along Agnes' tentacle, her veins popping blue with the strain. With one final enormous effort, Agnes pulled level with the rear guard of the Sisters. The bubble almost faded away to let through a freezing, roaring blast, but with one big krakeny breath, their safety sac renewed, held, and flashed brighter, maybe for attention, maybe for reassurance.

The song died in Cinrak's throat. Loquolchi faded to a breathy squeak. Benj pressed his face and paws against the elastic bubble, not caring that he leaned precariously over a drop that could end him if Agnes' strength gave out. Cinrak grabbed his forepaw out of a powerful storm-born instinct.

The rear star of the constellation was not one, but several bright beings, carousing krakens in close formation. Each being pulsed a different colour. They all had in common trailing tentacles and a castle-window sized single eye.

Those eyes were open, glazed with a crystal-like quality, staring at Agnes' and her passengers. Passengers who felt like motes of dust compared to the enormity of these kraken-stars and their journey.

Agnes fluoresced again and inserted herself into formation.

The Eight Sisters were Nine.

The kraken stars made no indication they knew Agnes was there.

Agnes tried all sorts of tricks, wriggling her other tentacles, flashing the bubble, intricate weavings between the stars. The three passengers sang as loud as they could, making a hatchet job of 'Perceive the Celestial Way', the opera's finale. Cinrak untied a length of the mer hair rope, tried interpretive dance, waved it about like a flag, skipped rope.

Nothing. The kraken-stars didn't blink. Their flight angle began to turn upwards and away.

How to touch a kraken-star heart? Cinrak desperately ran through her bags of tricks, all she knew about how to use her salty magic. Agnes pulsed in time with her siblings. Like a heart beat.

A heart! That's it!

One forepaw still clutching the mer hair rope, Cinrak reached into the Alice pocket of her vest and floundered through her chest of goodies under her bunk on the *Impolite Fortune*. A hard warmth nestled into her paw.

What if Xolotli's gift from so long ago wasn't a whale heart at all, but a kraken one!

Cinrak pulled the Heart of the Ocean free from her pocket. Its scintillating sapphire shot with resplendent ruby flashed in time with the krakens. Did it...float above her paw?

Then she was seeing the opposite of stars, black freckles slicking together like evil fire.

Out of breath, her passengers in various forms of exhausted disarray, Agnes angled towards the call of home.

She had given her all.

And her all had not been enough.

Everyone tumbled off the end of Agnes' tentacle, and Cinrak tripped to collapse face down in sand.

Back where they had begun.

Water whispered a sad tune to the islet's beach. The Paper Moon hid its face behind a wisp of cloud while the Moth Moon remained a staunch beacon.

Loquolchi lay on her back, staring up. Benj curled in on himself, listening to some far-off tune, breath hitching. Agnes bobbed a way off shore in a deep bay, only the tip of her spade head visible.

One final booming crack from above, and the light of the racing stars disappeared back down to their usual fine points.

Every piece of Cinrak ached, to the tips of each individual fur strand.

None of them said anything for a long time, watching the empty, betraying sky.

Cinrak cleared a sad crackle from her throat, determined to do what she always did as a captain: carry on. "The sky doesn't forget, nor it be immune to worldly worries, but sometimes it just doesn't care. An' we must be a'ight with that."

Loquolchi heaved a sigh. Benj remained still.

"Poor Agnes," Cinrak murmured. "I failed ye, ye poor mite."

A squidgy damp mass patted her on the chest. Cinrak chuckled wryly. Even mired in exhaustion, Agnes was trying to comfort her.

Cinrak patted the tentacle back. "Ye a good wee squiddy. We take care o' ya."

A harmonized gasp.

The exhausted mer hair rope coiled atop her jacket twitched. Cinrak lifted the heavy weight of one eyelid, then another, forehead wrinkling with surprise, cracking the crust of sand and ice.

The tentacle exploring her silk clothes, fur, and face was not orange, but a beautiful sunrise pink.

A second tentacle wriggled out of the water and patted Benj's leg. This one was the purple of a late summer's night.

More tentacles and colours washed the bay with a delicious luminescence, making the water ripple like a cave of hidden jewelled wonder. Crystal scales dissolved in the warm water and flaked off their enormous eyes. Those curious, all-seeing eyes blinked, scattering waves, startled dolphins, and birds.

The three mammals crawled to the water's edge, entranced, Benj reaching out a paw, unerringly finding an orange tentacle amongst the morass.

Her prim divaness dissolved, dress covered in wet sand, Loquolchi sobbed. It took effort for Cinrak to lift a stone-heavy arm to put around her love.

With her other forepaw, she patted down her person. The Heart of the Ocean was gone. Lost in midair, or a gratefully received gift?

Salacious Sharks! Cinrak dug back into her Alice pocket and tickled the kraken-spirit guarding her chest from it star-turns long slumber.

In all their star-turns working together, Cinrak had discovered they weren't *of* the kraken, but a symbiote sprite. They had been happy to stay in a pirate's employ as Agnes' had her own symbiote in Benj. Now was the sprite's opportunity to return to the life they loved most: keeping a kraken clean for the pleasure of travelling the "Great Dream," as they called it.

Cinrak held her Alice pocket open and with a trilling cry, the sprite slid out and latched on to the nearest kraken, a great blue. The blue wriggled with what could be read as happiness, if Agnes was anyone to go by.

She gave the sprite a salute for services well rendered.

"They came back." Benj finally found his words, tears making his voice deep and throaty, keeping the volume low as if afraid anything louder would scare the embrace of squiddies executing an intricate dance around their long-lost sibling. "They heard us. They—" he jerked as if touching one of those new electrickery wires the engineerers were playing with in the laboratories. "They love Agnes. They love *us*. That's an over-simplification, of course. I don't think I can touch their mind-speak without going a little mad, because what they know is—" He struggled to find an adequate word. "—astronomic."

They all managed a little chuckle. Loquolchi hiccuped.

Cinrak wiped the silent tears from her love's fur, then squeezed Benj's free forepaw. The chinchilla looked like he never wanted to let Agnes' tentacle go.

Agnes patted each of their cheeks, the huge tip of her tentacle gentle as a kiss. Cinrak had never wished for more magic than the little salt she possessed, but for a moment she wanted more than anything to touch the enormous intellect to express her thanks.

Agnes's tentacle wriggled a little. Somehow, she knew.

Lights flared along the spread of the islands to the east. The splash-down must have been observed. People would be coming. To rescue them. To observe. To wonder. To love.

And to fear the enormity of it all. Because there were always those who feared something larger, more intelligent, something that would threaten their power, even if that something was nowhere near that way inclined. It would be a hard task to explain how the kraken were back to *balance* the world, not take it over.

For a moment, they had the spectacle to themselves. Cinrak held her family tight, including Agnes' tentacle. All they had to do was watch the precious star-jewels swirl in the deep bay, and revel in the beautiful and terrifying and intricate change that was life.

ABOUT THE AUTHOR

A.J. FITZWATER CAN BE FOUND living between the cracks of Christchurch, New Zealand. They survived the Clarion workshop in 2014, added two Sir Julius Vogel Awards to their shelf, and have gone on to have work published in *Clarkesworld*, *Shimmer Magazine*, *Giganotosaurus*, *Beneath Ceaseless Skies*, *Glittership*, *Capricious Magazine*, and other venues and anthologies of repute. Their WW2 NZ Land Girls shape-shifter novella "No Man's Land" will be published by Paper Road Press in early 2020. They Twitter at @AJFitzwater.

ABOUT
QUEEN OF SWORDS
PRESS

QUEEN OF SWORDS IS an independent small press, specializing in swashbuckling tales of derring-do, bold new adventures in time and space, mysterious stories of the occult and arcane and fantastical tales of people and lands far and near. Visit us online at www. queenofswordspress.com and sign up for our mailing list to get notified about upcoming releases and offers. Or follow us on Facebook at the Queen of Swords Press page so you don't miss any press news.

If you have a moment, the author would appreciate you taking the time to leave a review for this book at Goodreads, your blog or on the site you purchased it from.

Thank you for your assistance and your support of our authors.

CPSIA information can be obtained
at www.ICGtesting.com
Printed in the USA
LVHW081203121120
671146LV00010B/331